Plains Warrior

CHIEF QUANAH PARKER AND THE COMANCHES

Books by Albert Marrin

The Airman's War
Overlord
Victory in the Pacific
The Secret Armies
The Sea Rovers
War Clouds in the West
Aztecs and Spaniards
The Yanks Are Coming
Struggle for a Continent
The War for Independence
Inca and Spaniard
The Spanish-American War
Cowboys, Indians, and Gunfighters
Unconditional Surrender: U.S. Grant and the Civil War
Virginia's General: Robert E. Lee and the Civil War
The Sea King: Sir Francis Drake and His Times
Plains Warrior: Chief Quanah Parker and the Comanches

Plains Warrior

CHIEF QUANAH PARKER AND THE COMANCHES

Albert Marrin

x x x x x x x x x x

ATHENEUM BOOKS FOR YOUNG READERS

Atheneum Books for Young Readers
An imprint of Simon & Schuster Children's Publishing Division
1230 Avenue of the Americas
New York, New York 10020

Book design by Edward Noriega

The text of this book is set in Janson Text.

Printed and bound in the United States of America

10 9 8 7 6 5 4 3 2 1

Library of Congress Cataloging-in-Publication Data

Plains warrior.
    p.   cm.
ISBN 0-689-80081-9 (hardcover)
1. Parker, Quanah, 1845?–1911—Juvenile literature.   2. Comanche Indians—
Biography—Juvenile literature.   3. Comanche Indians—Kings and rulers—
Juvenile literature.   4. Comanche Indians—History—Juvenile literature.
E99.C85P3864   1996
973'.04974—dc20
95-23048
CIP

Page 200 constitutes an extension of the copyright page and contains the photo
credits for this book.

Contents

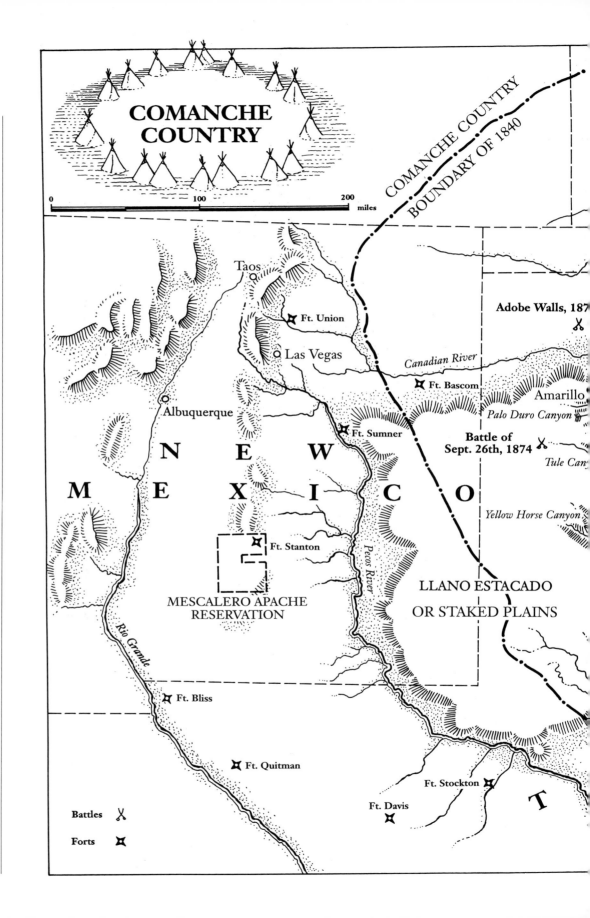

COMANCHE
COUNTRY

0   100   200
miles

COMANCHE COUNTRY
BOUNDARY OF 1840

Taos

✠ Ft. Union

Las Vegas

Adobe Walls, 187

Canadian River

✠ Ft. Bascom

Albuquerque

Amarillo

Palo Duro Canyon

✠ Ft. Sumner

**Battle of
Sept. 26th, 1874**

Tule Can

N E W

M E X I C O

Yellow Horse Canyon

✠ Ft. Stanton

Pecos River

MESCALERO APACHE
RESERVATION

LLANO ESTACADO

OR STAKED PLAINS

Rio Grande

✠ Ft. Bliss

✠ Ft. Quitman

Ft. Stockton ✠

Ft. Davis
✠

T

Battles   ⚔

Forts   ✠

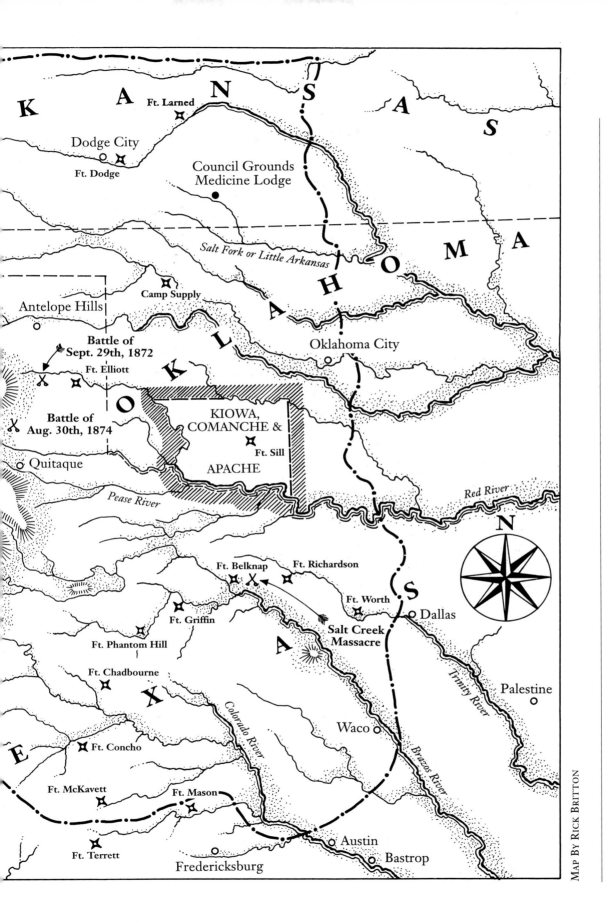

K A N S A S

Ft. Larned

Dodge City

Ft. Dodge

Council Grounds
Medicine Lodge

Salt Fork or Little Arkansas

Camp Supply

Antelope Hills

**Battle of
Sept. 29th, 1872**

Ft. Elliott

**Battle of
Aug. 30th, 1874**

Quitaque

OKLAHOMA

Oklahoma City

KIOWA,
COMANCHE &

APACHE

Ft. Sill

Pease River

Red River

N

Ft. Belknap   Ft. Richardson

Ft. Worth

Dallas

**Salt Creek
Massacre**

Ft. Griffin

Ft. Phantom Hill

Palestine

Trinity River

Ft. Chadbourne

T E X A S

Colorado River

Waco

Ft. Concho

Brazos River

Ft. McKavett

Ft. Mason

Ft. Terrett

Austin

Bastrop

Fredericksburg

Map By Rick Britton

"My mother raised me like your mothers raised their children, but my father taught me to be brave and learn to fight to become chief of my people."

—Chief Quanah Parker, July 1896

Cynthia Ann

"Comanches! Dreaded name. . . . What terror that name inspires along the defenseless frontier. And it was amongst these . . . that I had fallen a helpless victim."

—Ole Nystel, 1888

THURSDAY, May 19, 1836. A glorious spring morning with a cloudless sky of the bluest blue. The trees were in full leaf and the grass rippled, like ocean swells, in the gentle breeze. The scent of wildflowers filled the air, while birds chirped and chattered in their search for food and mates.

The residents of Fort Parker had been up, as usual, since before daybreak. The fort lay on the bank of the Navasota River, a branch of the Brazos, in Limestone County, Texas. This was frontier country, the spearhead of white settlement thrusting into the domain of the Plains Indians. Not that these settlers meant to harm anyone. They had come to Texas just two years earlier, by way of Virginia, Tennessee, and Illinois. Their leader was seventy-nine-year-old John Parker, a veteran of the American Revolution. A restless man, it seemed that he had spent his entire life searching for a promised land of peace and plenty. Known as Elder John to his followers, he was a leader of the Hardshell Baptists, a Protestant sect that believed in hard work, clean living, and following the Bible's teachings down to the very last word.

The Texas pioneers had moved westward in small family groupings. When they found a place that suited them, they built their settlements. The land was so vast, and the pioneers so few, that it felt as if they were the only humans on earth. Settlements were so isolated that it took many hours, even days, to travel from one to another even on horseback. The Parkers and the families that joined them cleared the woods near their new home, pulled up the tree stumps with teams of oxen, and began farming the rich soil. For protection, they "forted up."

Protection was vital, since they had moved into a dangerous borderland. The "horse Indians" who roamed the plains to the north, west, and southwest resented anyone who came near their hunting grounds—and they were not folk to be toyed with. Fort Parker had been laid out with this fact in mind. Each family had its own log cabin, the whole surrounded by a stockade of logs set close together in the ground and pointed at the top. Entry to the stockade was through a bulletproof gate made of heavy wooden slabs swinging on hinges. Blockhouses were built at the corners, giving added protection. Each blockhouse had two floors; the lower floor served as a storage area, and the upper floor, reached only by ladder from inside, was a strong defensive position. As an added precaution, the upper floor was eighteen inches larger than the one beneath, with portholes for shooting attackers who tried to use the walls for cover.

Fort Parker's inhabitants were independent folks, who needed no government to give purpose and meaning to their lives. All they wanted was the right to earn their living from the soil and worship God in their own way. Each day was like every other. They praised the Lord, did their chores, and minded their own business. Their routines were set, as regular and unvarying as the sun in its daily journey across the sky. Nothing short of a major disaster could make them do anything differently.

Such a disaster had occurred a few weeks earlier. Texas was a Mexican province into which Americans had been invited fifteen years before. In 1836, however, the settlers revolted against the dictator General Antonio López de Santa Anna. Events moved swiftly. On March 2, Texas declared itself an independent republic. Four days later, the Mexican army stormed the Alamo, a fortified mission in San Antonio, killing all 187 of its defenders, including those who tried to surrender. Among the dead were the famous frontiersmen Jim Bowie and Davy Crockett. But Santa Anna's victory was short-lived. On April 21, the Texas army under General Sam Houston won a brilliant victory at the Battle of San Jacinto. The battle ended the war, and Texas won its independence as a separate country.

The men of Fort Parker took no part in the fighting; indeed, the entire settlement had fled at the enemy's approach. When word came of the victory at San Jacinto, families returned to their homes as if nothing had happened. Everything was back to normal by May 19. Thirty-one people were inside the fort that morning: ten women, fifteen children, and six men; another three men were working in the fields a mile away. They felt so safe that, apparently, no one noticed that the gate had been left wide open.

Nine-year-old Cynthia Ann Parker was the daughter of Silas Parker, Elder John's oldest son, and his wife, Lucy. Fair-skinned and blue-eyed, with light brown hair, she was feeding the chickens when, at about eight o'clock, there was a startled cry.

"Indians! Indians!" someone called. Looking up, she saw anywhere from one hundred to five hundred Indians—the exact number is uncertain—in the clearing outside the gate. It was as if they had sprung from the earth, so quietly had they come. They sat on their horses, motionless, practically naked, their faces and bodies painted with circles, lines, and zigzags, staring at the settlers. They were Comanches, joined by a few dozen Kiowas and Wichitas. Each carried a lance, a tomahawk, and a bow and arrows. One brave carried a white flag as a sign of peace.

Benjamin Parker, Silas's unmarried brother, came out to show that the whites were friendly. Speaking Spanish, a language most Texas Indians understood, he asked what they wanted. A chief replied that they needed food and directions to the nearest water hole. Benjamin returned to the fort, promising to be back in a few minutes. But he was worried—very worried. The Indians' requests, he told those anxiously crowding around him, made no sense. Why should they need a water hole when they had the Navasota? Surely they knew the river was nearby; indeed, their horses were wet up to the shoulders, proof that they had recently crossed a stream. Still, he returned to speak further with the horsemen. Meantime, one of the women slipped through a small rear gate to tell the men in the fields to come quickly with their muskets.

It was too late. As Benjamin approached the Indians, they spurred their horses forward. While some clubbed and speared him to death, the others swarmed through the open gate. What followed was fifteen minutes of pure terror. The noise was horrifying, a blend of war whoops, shrieks of pain, cries for mercy, and the thud of arrows striking flesh. Breaking into the log cabins, the raiders slashed open featherbeds, scattering their contents to make a May "blizzard." Medicine bottles and jars of preserves were smashed to bits.

Panicky women and children ran past the Indians toward the woods beyond. Their men, desperately trying to cover their retreat, were killed, scalped, and their bodies mutilated. Five died: three Parkers—Benjamin, Silas, Elder John—and two men from another family. Granny Parker, Elder John's wife, was pinned to the ground by a lance through her body and raped repeatedly. Five of the settlers were captured.

Mrs. Elizabeth Kellogg was the first to be seized; a warrior leaned down, grabbed her arms, and pulled her onto the saddle behind him. Mrs. Rachel Plummer and her fifteen-month-old son, James Pratt, were taken as they came through the rear gate. She described the experience in a heartbreaking book, *Rachel Plummer's Narrative, or Twenty-Two Months Servitude as a Prisoner Among the Comanche Indians*, first printed in 1839. As she ran out of the fort, her son in her arms, Rachel saw the Indians killing Benjamin Parker. Moments later, several braves cut off her retreat. "A large sulky looking Indian picked up a hoe and knocked me down," she recalled. "The first I recollect, they were dragging me along by the

hair. . . . I was soon dragged to the main body of Indians where they had killed Uncle Benjamin. His face was much mutilated and many arrows were sticking in his body. As the savages passed by, they thrust their spears through him."[1] Rachel was separated from her son, and both carried away behind mounted warriors.

Meanwhile, Lucy Parker was trying to escape with her four children. It was slow going, and the raiders overtook them at the edge of the woods. They had just lifted the children onto their horses when one of the men who had been working in the fields appeared. Pointing his musket at the Indians, he forced them to let go of the two youngest children. One brave, however, galloped away with Cynthia Ann and her brother, six-year-old John.

What were the raiders' names? Why did they strike? Who killed the men of Fort Parker and seized the captives? These questions are impossible to answer, and we shall never know the

Comanche raiders strike, seizing a white woman for ransom or marriage and cattle for food. From a drawing in *Harper's Weekly*, May 1, 1858.

full story of that awful day. Much of the history of the American West is, and must forever remain, one-sided. The reason is quite simple: Indians did not have a written language. Their accounts of events were preserved—if they were preserved at all—in the form of stories told by braves seeking war honors. When the storytellers died, or other matters occupied listeners' attention, the memory of the original event quickly faded. The whites, however, wrote down their experiences. This ability allowed them not only to record the past, but to control how it would be viewed by future generations. Thus, the history we have is essentially the conquerors' story, seen through their eyes and told with their pens.

All that is certain is that the Fort Parker captives survived their ordeal. And all but Cynthia Ann returned to their homes after a fairly short captivity. She would spend a quarter of a century with the Comanches.

These were the first American women and children known to have been taken by the Texas Indians. Cynthia Ann became a legend in her own time. Her disappearance stirred the frontier people's imagination. The story of her kidnapping was told and retold at firesides. Newspapers printed reports (generally false) of her being seen in various places. There was constant speculation about how she was getting along with the Comanches. Mothers warned rowdy youngsters that "the Comanches will take you away," like Cynthia Ann, if they misbehaved. Her memory is still very much alive in the twentieth century. *Cynthia Ann*, an opera by Julia Smith, was performed in 1939. In 1956, actor John Wayne starred in *The Searchers*, a movie about a Texan who sets out to rescue his two nieces from the Comanches, based on the novel by Alan Le May.

It is also certain that the Fort Parker raid was the first act of a tragedy that would play itself out over the next two generations. The years 1836 to 1875 were a time of ceaseless conflict in the Southwest. The Parker saga is a chapter in the "winning of the West," a glamorous term denoting color, excitement, and adventure. It was all of these—at times. Mostly, however, it was a savage contest between Indians and whites with neither side showing or expecting mercy.

The winning of the West was not a struggle between massed armies, but a guerrilla war of raids, ambushes, and massacres carried out by both sides. Measured in terms of the lives lost, its cost was low. Scholars believe that the United States Army killed fewer than three thousand Indians during all the Indian wars since 1776; white civilians may have killed an additional thousand.[2] These losses were less than one day's fighting in any of the major battles of the Civil War. Yet, in terms of human values—kindness, decency, generosity—the winning of the West was probably the most savage struggle in our history. At stake was nothing less than control of the vast territory between the Mississippi River and the Rocky Mountains.

Cynthia Ann was to play an unexpected role in this drama. Her Comanche captors refused to return her to her family, and no amount of ransom could persuade them to let her go. Nor did she wish to return. She quickly adapted to her new surroundings, until it seemed that she had always been with the Comanche. She *became* a Comanche—a "white Indian"—and married a Comanche war chief with whom she had three children.

Her firstborn son, Quanah, eventually became a chief in his own right. Quanah's life spanned some of the most dramatic, and tragic, years in American history. For nearly a century, his people defended their land in the southern part of the Great Plains. They were finally defeated, but what a fight they fought! Pioneers, settlers, Texas Rangers, cowboys, soldiers, buffalo hunters, the United States government: all had done their best to bring them down, but none could have succeeded alone. It took all of them together to end the Comanche's free life.

Our job is twofold. First, we must understand Quanah's people, the Comanche. Second, we must see how he led them in battle, finally bringing them to terms with defeat and helping them along the bumpy trail they called "the white man's road."

George Catlin's portrait of Little Spaniard, a famous Comanche war chief. The Comanche and their Kiowa allies were the fiercest and most feared warriors of the Southern Plains.

The People

"The civilized world looks upon a group of Indians . . . and laughs at them excessively, because they are not like ourselves. We ask, 'why do the silly creatures wear such great bunches of quills on their heads?—such loads and streaks of paint upon their bodies?—and bear's grease? abominable!' and a thousand other equally silly questions, without stopping to think that *Nature taught them* to do so—and that they all have some definite importance or meaning which the Indian could explain to us at once, *if* he were asked and felt disposed to do so. . . ."

—George Catlin, *North American Indians*, 1844

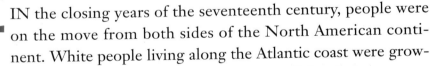

IN the closing years of the seventeenth century, people were on the move from both sides of the North American continent. White people living along the Atlantic coast were growing restless as the colonies filled with fresh arrivals from Europe. Like their ancestors before them, they spoke of America as the New World, a place of new beginnings where hard work could bring prosperity regardless of one's humble origins. So, from Georgia to Maine, pioneers, eager for land and opportunity, struck out westward across the Appalachian Mountains.

Far to the west, a new world was also being discovered by certain Native Americans. Among them were the Shoshone who lived in the Rocky Mountains, near the headwaters of the Yellowstone River. The Shoshone were a typical mountain people. Short, squat, and heavyset, their average height was five feet six inches for men and five feet for women. They had copper-colored skins, broad faces, thin lips, black or dark brown eyes, and jet-black hair. They had no metal, and used tools made of flint and bone. Nomads, lacking even a word for "home," they had always wandered the mountains and high meadows seeking food. They lived by hunting mountain deer, gathering nuts and berries, and digging roots. They had never planted a seed, woven a piece of cloth, or made a clay pot.

About the year 1690, the Shoshone were in the eastern Rockies, in the country called Wyoming. They had come to hunt, and meant, as always, to return to their familiar campsites. This time, however, things did not go as planned. Legend has it that a boy from one band accidentally killed a playmate from another, and that the slain boy's band wanted revenge. According to another story, two bands could not agree on sharing the game they had killed. Whatever the reason, some Shoshone decided not to go back to the mountains. To show that the break was final, they changed their name to Nerm, "True Human Beings," or "The People" for short. Later, they began to hunt with the Ute, distant cousins from southern Colorado. But again something went wrong. The Ute began calling them *Komántcia*, "Those Who Fight Us All the Time." The Spanish learned the name from the Ute and wrote it as *Commanche*. The Americans shortened it to *Comanche*. And for them all, Comanche meant enemy.

The People moved southward, surviving on small game and an occasional buffalo. By 1705, they had reached northwestern Texas, a flat, open country where sky and earth meet in a straight line on the horizon. There they found a new world. We call it the Great Plains.

Geologists, scientists who study the earth, tell us that the Great Plains was formed millions of years ago by melting snows from the Rocky Mountains. Soil and stones were swept down steep slopes by rivers flowing eastward into the Mississippi River a thousand miles away. As the rivers rushed out of the mountains, they lost speed, releasing their loads into their channels. The channel bottoms slowly rose, causing the rivers to overflow either to the right or left until they found new channels, repeating the process countless times. As a result, the land east of the mountains gradually filled in to form a single downward-sloping plain.

The slope is so gentle that it is not noticed in most places.

The Great Plains stretch from the eastern foothills of the Rockies to the Mississippi and from Mexico into Canada, an area covering one-third of the United States. Today, they include parts of ten states: Colorado, Kansas, Montana, Nebraska, New Mexico, North Dakota, Oklahoma, South Dakota, Texas, and Wyoming. Two large cities sit on its edges, Denver, Colorado, and San Antonio, Texas. The largest city on the Plains is Lubbock, Texas, with a population of nearly two hundred thousand.

The Plains are of two types. The Low or Rolling Plains tilt gently to the east and are cut by shallow rivers whose valleys contain rich soil and timber. The High Plains of northwestern Texas, also known as the Texas Panhandle, rise three thousand feet above sea level. Spanish explorers named the most striking part of this area the Llano Estacado or "Staked Plain," possibly because they hammered stakes into the ground so as not to lose their way. The Staked Plain is a gigantic plateau towering above the surrounding countryside. Larger than all of New England, it is as flat as a billiard table, except on its eastern edge, where rivers have cut deep canyons such as the Tule, Quitaque, Blanco, and Palo Duro.

Plains weather can be wonderful or dreadful, and everything in between. At its best, it is mild and refreshing, making it a joy to be alive. Wind is the problem; it blows constantly, usually with a force equal to that on the seashore. More than one white settler was driven crazy by the constant howling. "Does the wind blow this way here all the time?" a visitor once asked. "No, Mister," a Texan replied. "It'll blow this way for a week or ten days, and then it'll take a change and blow like hell for a while."[1]

Since there are no high hills to block them, the winds blow freely. In July and August, they blow from the deserts of Mexico and Arizona. These hot, dry winds are like a blowtorch. They send temperatures soaring to over a hundred degrees in the shade, withering plants, drying up streams, and causing animals to die of thirst. Dust devils, whirling funnels of soil rising hundreds of feet into the air, turn day into night. From early fall to early spring, "northers," cold Arctic winds, scour the Plains, sending temperatures plummeting twenty-five degrees in a few minutes and causing snow to fall a foot an hour. For variety, the Plains may be battered by hailstorms, cloudbursts, electrical storms, tornadoes, and prairie fires able to outrace an Olympic runner. When fire comes, every living thing above ground must either run, dig, or die. Fires burn hundreds of square miles, until checked by a stream or barren ground. Still, fire is beneficial, since it clears dead vegetation and produces ashes to fertilize the soil. Droughts come, too, and may last a year, a disaster since the Plains seldom get more than twenty inches of rain in any twelve-month period.

The Plains are covered with grass—short grass in the west, long grass in the east. Europeans were astonished upon first seeing the area. How different it was from anything they had known in the Old World! They were used to tree-covered hillsides and thick forests, places with natural boundaries and landmarks. The Plains, however, were limitless and monotonous; they seem to go on forever. And just as water closes in behind a ship, leaving no trace of its passing, so the grass closed in behind people. An army could trample it down, and it would spring back as if it had never been touched. In 1540 Francisco Vásquez de Coronado led an expedition across the Llano Estacado. "Who would believe," a soldier wrote, "that a thousand horses and five hundred of our cows and more than five thousand rams and ewes and more than fifteen hundred friendly Indians and servants, in traveling over those plains, would leave no more trace where they had passed than if nothing had been there—nothing—so that it was necessary to make piles of bones and cow dung now and then, so that the rear guard could follow the army."[2]

Plains grass sent its roots down at least twenty-four inches, making it practically drought-proof; fire burned everything above ground, but did not harm the grasses' roots, which soon produced a fresh growth. Because of it, the Plains teemed with deer, elk, antelope, jackrabbits, and prairie dogs, a ground squirrel that lived in "towns" numbering in the millions. These animals ate the grass, and the flesh-eaters—coyotes, wolves, bears—ate them. But the king of the Plains was the American bison, or buffalo, of which there were between sixty and seventy-five million when Europeans first set foot in the New World.

After conquering Mexico in 1521, Hernan Cortés found several buffalo in the private zoo of the Aztec ruler, Montezuma. These "hump-backed oxen" were fantastic creatures. "In shape and form they are so marvelous and laughable, or frightful, that the more one sees of it the more one desires to see it," a Spaniard wrote.

> Its horns are black . . . its eyes are small, its face, snout, feet, and hoofs of the same form as our cows, with the exception that both the male and female are very much bearded, similar to he-goats. They are so thickly covered with wool that it covers their eyes and face, and the forelock nearly envelops their horns. This wool, which is very long and very soft, extends almost to the middle of the body, but from there on the hair is shorter. . . . Their tail is like that of a hog, being very short, and having few bristles at the tip, and they twist it upward when they run. At the knee they have natural garters of very long hair. . . . They are all of the same dark color, somewhat tawny, in parts their hair being almost black. Such is their appearance, which in sight is far more ferocious than the pen can depict.[3]

A relative of the cow, goat, and antelope, the buffalo was the largest land animal in the New World. An adult bull stood six feet at the shoulders, was nine and one-half feet long, and weighed from 2,000 to 2,600 pounds; full-grown cows weighed anywhere from 1,200 to 1,500 pounds. These animals were four-legged mowing machines. In order to keep going, they had to eat thirty pounds of grass a day. Yet they were small compared to their ancestors of four hundred thousand years ago. These monsters were more than twice as big, with a forty-inch spread of horns from tip to tip.

Weather was the buffalo's worst natural enemy. Lightning strikes killed dozens of animals standing close together. Prairie fires burned them by the thousands, or stampeded them off cliffs. Crossing rivers covered with thin ice sent them to watery graves a hundred thousand at a time. The funnel clouds of tornadoes dipped into herds, lifting buffaloes into the air and then slamming them back down onto the earth. One tornado piled their bodies five deep, one on top of another, in a straight line for a quarter of a mile. Many were stripped of their hair, with their eyes torn out by the wind's suction, hanging down their faces. Meat eaters, by comparison, did them little harm. Packs of wolves followed the herds, preying on the very young and the very old. But wolves were no match for a full-grown buffalo in the prime of life. More than one wolf had its belly torn open by the slashing horns.

The buffalo moved in immense herds. Astonished travelers estimated that some herds contained upward of two million animals, and these were nothing special. A really large herd might be a solidly packed mass fifty miles deep and twenty-five miles wide. Such a herd would thunder past a fixed point for a week, carving a deep trail with their hooves.

At the time of the American Revolution, buffalo ranged from the Blue Mountains of Oregon clear across the continent to the western portions of New York, Pennsylvania, Virginia, the Carolinas, and Georgia. The largest herds, however, roamed the High Plains of Texas. Though the wild herds disappeared over a century ago, they live on in certain place names. Texas has at least a dozen streams named Buffalo Creek and a town called Buffalo Springs. There is also a Buffalo Gap, a Buffalo Lake, a Buffalo Peak, and a Buffalo Point. Without the buffalo, the story of the West would have been entirely different.

✕   ✕   ✕

Indians had inhabited the Plains river valleys for centuries. Tribes lived in scattered villages, growing beans, squash, and corn in small gardens tended by women. Few ventured far out onto the Plains themselves, or stayed very long if they did. The open Plains were awesome. The sea of grass stretched before them, apparently limitless, making them feel tiny and insignificant. Worse, the Plains were the domain of Thunderbird, god of storms, who darkened the sky with clouds and pelted the earth with hailstones the size of a man's fist. Thunderbird's lightning fired the grass and made the buffalo stampede, trampling every-thing in their path. Only hunger, a force stronger than fear, could draw the Indians out of their valleys.

After the crops were planted and before the harvest, entire villages moved onto the Plains to hunt buffalo. It was not easy. Although the buffalo had poor eyesight, it had a keen sense of smell. The slightest hint of man-scent would send a herd pound-ing away at thirty miles an hour. The Indians could not follow close behind a herd as it moved from one grazing spot to anoth-er. They had no means of transportation other than their own legs and their dogs, wolflike creatures that constantly fought among themselves. When a family moved, its belongings were placed on a travois, a platform fastened between two long poles, one end of each tied to a dog's shoulders, the other dragging behind on the ground. A strong dog could pull twenty pounds at most.

Various methods were used to kill buffalo. Sometimes a fire was set around a herd, hemming in the animals except for a nar-row exit, where the hunters waited with their bows and arrows. Another method was to stampede a herd over a cliff, or "buffalo jump," killing the animals outright or crippling them so that the hunters could finish the job. Occasionally, hunters came upon buffaloes that had sunk up to their bellies in a muddy riverbank; these were an easy kill. But if hunters did not find them, the trapped animals starved to death. An explorer once saw from a distance several hundred buffaloes standing perfectly still along a riverbank. Moving closer, he found them all stiff and dead. They had dried up in the dry Plains air without rotting.[4]

Living on the Plains was difficult at the best of times. Since water might be hard to find, hunters refilled "canteens" after each kill. "They empty a large gut and fill it with blood," a Spaniard wrote, "and carry it about their necks to drink when thirsty."[5] Winter, however, was the worst season. Cold was usually not a serious problem; tribes sheltered in the river valleys and canyons, escaping the frigid northers. Hunger was another matter. By late winter, food supplies were getting dangerously low. The harvest was nearly used up, and no one dared venture far on the snow-covered Plains. No wonder they called February and March the "starving time" and the "time when our babies cry for food." Desperate people ate anything: snakes, skunks, rats, lizards, tree bark. If even these were scarce, old people and infants were abandoned to save food for those best able to carry on the life of the tribe. Scientists have found cracked and charred human bones at some ancient campsites, indicating cannibalism.

The horse changed everything. Horses had once existed in the New World, disappearing about seven thousand years ago. The Spaniards reintroduced the horse in the early 1500s. The Spanish horse was something special. Of a type known as the barb, it was strong, hardy, and alert. Unlike the heavy, grain-fed horses of Western Europe, the barb was small and wiry, weighing no more than seven hundred pounds. Built for speed, it had a slender neck, long legs, and a long mane and tail. Brought to Spain from North Africa during the Middle Ages, it could go great distances without water and feed entirely on grass. It was at home in Mexico and the grasslands to the north.

Horses, not guns, enabled the conquistadores to work miracles on the battlefield. The Aztecs had huge armies of foot soldiers armed with spears and clubs edged with razor-sharp flints. Yet they were no match for a mounted Spaniard. A man wearing steel armor could not fight well on foot; it slowed him down and weighed him down. But a man on a horse was irresistible. A charge, even by a few horsemen, struck with such force that it easily plowed through the Indian ranks, spreading panic. Once the enemy was on the run, riders came up from behind, swinging their swords and leaving a trail of headless bodies.

Spaniards pushed northward into New Mexico in the 1590s. New Mexico was home to the Pueblo Indians, farmers who lived in villages (pueblos) of three- and four-story "apartment" houses built of stone and adobe, bricks of sun-dried clay. The invaders wanted three things: to convert the Indians to Christianity, to find gold and silver, and to take slaves to work for Spanish masters. They believed they were acting in everyone's best interests. *Los Indios*, Spaniards insisted, were *gente sin razón*—"people without reason." Mindless savages, they could only become truly human by becoming Christians and serving their "betters."

Indians who resisted paid a heavy price, as the people of Acoma learned to their regret. Acoma pueblo, or Sky City because of its location atop a flat-topped hill known as a mesa, was a natural fortress. But when the Acomans rebelled in 1598, the Spanish stormed their defenses, killing eight hundred in a single day. The governor made an example of the survivors. Every Acoma man over the age of twenty-five had one foot chopped off and was enslaved for twenty years. Boys between twelve and twenty-five and women over twelve were sentenced to twenty years of slavery. Children under twelve were given to Spanish families to be raised as Christians. Two Hopi Indians, who were in Acoma during the battle, became prisoners. The Spanish commander sentenced them "to have the right hand cut off and to be set free in order that they convey to their land the news of this punishment."[6]

The conquerors settled among the Pueblos on farms and ranches, forcing them to tend their crops and livestock. Though Spanish law forbade Indians to ride horses, not to mention own them, it was impossible to manage herds of cattle on foot. So the law was ignored, and soon Indian cowboys, or *vaqueros*, were working cattle on horseback. Discipline was strict. *Vaqueros* who fell down on the job, or missed church services, were fined and whipped. Such brutality, however, backfired. Every year scores of

Vaqueros in a Corral. Painted by James Walker in 1877, this picture shows Mexican cowboys, one of whom is roping a horse. Magnificent riders, Mexicans originally taught many of the Plains Indian tribes the fine points of horsemanship.

vaqueros ran away; actually, they rode away, taking horses and horse knowledge with them. They went to the "wild" Indians—Navajos and Apaches—in the hills and along the western fringes of the Great Plains. To the Spaniards, these were wild men, because they refused to be "tamed." Particularly the Apache, who lived in farming communities called *rancherías* (Spanish for "small villages") and hunted buffalo in their spare time. The Pueblos taught their friends everything they knew about horses. They taught them how to ride and care for horses. They also taught them how to make riding gear: stirrups out of forked sticks, harness out of leather strips, lariats out of braided rawhide, saddles out of leather bags stuffed with straw. And they taught them how to steal horses. By 1650, bands of wild Indians were creeping up to corrals and waving blankets to run off the horses.

To tighten their control, the Spaniards doubled taxes and forbade travel from one pueblo to another without an official pass. By 1680, the Pueblos had had enough. They rebelled and drove the invaders out of New Mexico for twelve years. The Spaniards, caught by surprise, abandoned their homes in such haste that they left nearly all of their possessions behind. Other

than the cattle and sheep, which they ate, the rebels had little use for most of these things.

Horses, however, were something else. Thousands were taken for the Pueblos' own use or to trade with distant tribes. Thousands of others broke free, scattering to the Plains, where, without natural enemies, they multiplied. Within a generation, horse herds were roaming the plains of eastern New Mexico and Texas along the Rio Grande. Spaniards called them *mesteños*, or "strays." From this we get the English word "mustang."

Year by year, horses passed northward. As the New Mexico tribes acquired horses, they sold or traded spare mounts to their neighbors and shared their horse knowledge. The Kiowa were riding by 1682, the Pawnee by 1700, the Crow and Lakota (Sioux) by 1742. The Ute had introduced their Comanche cousins to the horse by 1714, before they began feuding. By 1784, tribes from Mexico to Canada were mounted. The effect was electrifying. Within a century, thirty tribes abandoned their sheltered river valleys and moved permanently onto the Great Plains. Farming was forgotten. For 175 years, they were "horse Indians" and buffalo hunters. Those years, 1700 to 1875, would be proudly remembered as a golden age.

Seldom has an animal brought about such a sudden and complete change in the life of a people. The horse was to the Plains Indians what steamboats, railroads, automobiles, and airplanes would be to whites. They called the horse "Holy Dog," "Mystery Dog," and "Spirit Dog." And for good reason, since such a marvelous creature could only have been a gift from the Great Spirit. There can be no understanding of the Plains Indians, and most of all the Comanche, without an understanding of their relationship to the horse.

The horse enabled the Indians to travel in ways they had never imagined. Now they could boldly venture anywhere on the grass sea. What used to be a week's journey on foot took less than a day on horseback. They could follow the buffalo herds, which in turn put an end to hunger, causing population to rise. No

Tricks of the trade. Comanche warriors could hang over the saddles of their mounts, using them as moving shields during a battle. This drawing is by George Catlin.

longer was it necessary to take only the barest necessities; a horse-drawn travois could move a hundred pounds of baggage, and do it easily. Best of all, the horse changed the Indians' outlook. Mastery of the horse meant self-mastery, confidence in their ability to control their destiny. It was a good feeling.

No Indians took to the horse so easily and so completely as The People, who owned more horses than any other Plains tribe. A Sioux war chief, for instance, considered himself wealthy if he had 40 horses; an ordinary Comanche warrior owned 250, and a war chief 1,500. A Comanche band of fewer than two thousand people owned 15,000 horses and 400 mules! The entire Pawnee tribe had 1,400 horses, the Osage 1,200, and the Omaha 1,200. [7]

There were no horsemen on earth like The People. Everyone—men, women, and children—rode as easily as they walked. Whites who saw them in their heyday could scarcely believe their eyes. All agreed that they were among the best, if not *the* best, riders who had ever lived. Baldwin Möllhausen, a German scientist who toured the West in the 1850s, said the Comanche was born to the saddle. "Indeed, he makes but an awkward figure enough on foot, though he is no sooner mounted than he is transformed; and when with no other aid than that of the rein and a heavy whip he makes his horse perform the most incredible feats."[8]

Hundreds of hours were invested in a horse's training. The result was a mount that instantly responded to a command. A Comanche horse could stop in its own length while galloping at full speed or turn sharply in a circle, guided only by the pressure of its rider's knees. A warrior could swing over one side of his mount and use its body as a shield. By hooking a leg over the horse's back and hanging by a loop of buffalo hair woven into its mane, he could shoot arrows from under its neck while speeding across the Plains.

Horses were a warrior's most prized possessions. His favorite mount was kept picketed close to his tipi at night, or tied to his wrist by a six-foot rope while he slept. He cared for it, caressed it, spoke to it, loved it; some men, it was said, loved their horses more than their wives and children. Killing a man's favorite horse was like murder, calling for revenge against the killer's horse—or his body. Like automobiles among latter-day Americans, horses were an emotional subject with The People, causing more than one fight to the death.

The People could also be cruel to their beloved horses, if necessary. Texans, no mean judges of horseflesh, had a saying: "A white man will ride a horse until he is played out; a Mexican will

Drawn by George Catlin in 1834, this depicts Comanche braves capturing horses from one of the countless herds of mustangs, or wild horses, that roamed the Great Plains.

abandon him after riding him another fifty miles; then a Comanche will ride him for a week." A Comanche would ride a horse whose back was raw and bleeding from an ill-fitting saddle, then, when it dropped from exhaustion, force it to get up and keep going.

Stealing from other tribes was the preferred method of obtaining horses. The People were the world's champion horse thieves. They could slip into a village at night, cut the rope on a sleeping owner's wrist, and be gone without waking a soul. So skilled were they that pioneers believed they put a spell on animals, making even watchdogs lose their voice while they emptied the corrals; not even roosters crowed when Comanches were about! Next to stealing, the mustang herds were their main source of fresh mounts. Mustangs were chased on the open range and captured with lariats, or ambushed near water holes after they had drunk their fill and their sagging bellies prevented them from galloping away at top speed.

Mustangs were quickly tamed, or broken. "Broken" is the right word, since the horse was forced to learn who was master in a very short time. First it was choked with a lariat and, when it could no longer resist, thrown to the ground. The brave then tied a pair of hobbles onto its forelegs, looped a rope around its lower jaw and tied it around its neck, finally blowing his breath into its

A Plains Indian village on the move, as recorded by George Catlin. Here members of the group try to break up a dogfight.

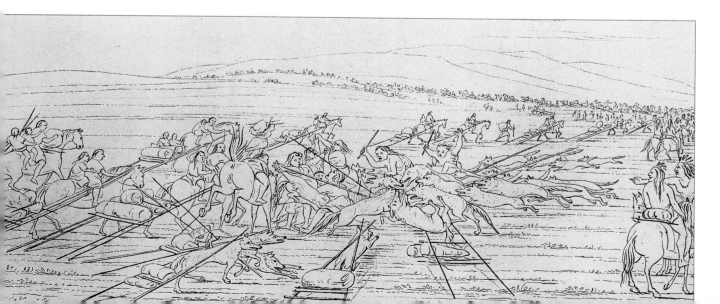

nostrils. This calmed the horse, while showing who was in charge. After a few days, the brave rode his mustang for the first time in a deep stream to keep it from bucking too high. Mustangs were not shod; Plains Indians did not have iron horseshoes. Instead, its hooves were hardened by walking it back and forth near a hot fire.

The horse turned The People into full-time buffalo hunters. The Comanche found it easier to hunt over a wide area in separate bands rather than as a unified tribe. Thirteen bands were known, most of them with fewer than a thousand members each. Among the smaller bands were those with names like "Hill Wearing Away," "Sunshades on Their Backs," and "Those with Maggots on the Penis"; the meaning of these names has been lost. There were five major bands. The largest, the *Penateka* ("Honey-Eaters"), lived farthest south, in Texas. To its north were the *Nokoni* ("Wanderers"), who hunted on either side of the Red River. The *Kotsoteka* ("Buffalo-Eaters") lived to the north of these, and the *Yamparika* ("Eaters of the Yampa Root") furthest north, between the Cimarron and Arkansas Rivers. The *Quahadi* ("Antelopes") roamed the Staked Plain. Any Comanche was free to leave one band and go to another, if it would have him. In all, The People numbered between fifteen and twenty thousand in the early 1800s.[9]

The buffalo was The People's staff of life—their food, their clothing, their shelter, their tools. They worshiped it as a guardian spirit who, if they acted properly, would always support them generously. When the sacred pipe was smoked during religious ceremonies, a puff was blown into a buffalo skull, along with a thankful prayer. Sometimes a buffalo spoke to a person, even turned into a human being, to reveal a herd's location. All Plains Indians believed that the Great Spirit produced buffaloes in countless numbers in underground caverns called "buffalo holes." Every spring, just as the bees began to swarm, the buffalo emerged from two openings in the Staked Plain. There were so many of them that The People would be able to hunt them forever without reducing their numbers, they believed. Surely, it was impossible to exterminate the buffalo. The very idea was ridiculous, foolish, unthinkable.

Buffalo flesh, although coarser and darker than beef, was tasty and nutritious. White travelers enjoyed it as much as the Indians. Zebulon Montgomery Pike, discoverer of Pikes Peak in Colorado, wrote in his diary on November 6, 1806: "The cow buffalo was equal to any meat I ever saw, and we feasted sumptuously on the choice morsels." The naturalist John James Audubon preferred buffalo meat to beef.[10]

The People used every part of the buffalo. Beginning with the head and working backward, they wasted nothing. Its skull was placed near camp as a sign of respect and to "attract" other buffaloes. Its horns made handy cups, spoons, ladles, and fire carriers; not having matches, The People carried live coals from one campsite to another, rather than start fire each time by rubbing sticks together. Buffalo beards ornamented clothing and weapons; hair became paintbrushes, stuffing for cradleboards, gloves, and pillows, and was woven into rope. Sinew, a fiber lying along the spine, became sewing thread, cinches, and bowstrings. Tanned hide was made into dozens of items: robes, blankets, saddlebags, pouches, belts, leggings, hats, dresses, shirts, cradles, drums, tipi covers. Untanned hide, called "rawhide," became lariats and parfleches, leather envelopes used to store everything from food to spare clothes. Bones were shaped into needles, flesh scrapers, awls, knife blades, and ornaments. The skin of the hind legs was peeled off in one piece for moccasins and boots. Boiled hooves produced glue for attaching feathers to arrows. The bull's scrotum served as a rattle. The heart was left intact, so that the buffalo's spirit might return in the body of another animal.

Buffalo manure also had its uses. Tons of "buffalo chips," pats the size of a man's hand, accumulated wherever the herds passed. Even when they were wet on the outside, they stayed dry inside, making them an ideal fuel for cooking and heating. More, The People used them during religious ceremonies to keep sacred objects from touching the ground. Indeed, buffalo chips were sacred in themselves; braves swore they were telling the truth on a pile of manure.

The main buffalo hunts were held in the summer and early fall. If a herd was nowhere to be seen, a horned toad was asked where it was. The People believed the toad would go off in the direction of the nearest herd. Perhaps it did. Still, the raven was a surer guide. Ravens followed the herds to eat the insects clinging to the animals' hides and to feast on the dead. Flocks of ravens circling in the distance were a sure sign of buffalo below.

Buffalo meat was the Plains Indians' basic food. Here strips of meat are hanging from a rack to be jerked, or dried, by the wind.

Buffalo Hunt, by
Charles M. Russell.
Known as the
"cowboy artist,"
Russell painted
highly accurate
pictures of Native
American and white
frontier life.

When a herd was sighted, the hunters prepared for a "sur-round." Moving slowly, they formed a wide arc along one side of the herd, taking care to stay downwind as long as possible. At the leader's signal, they whipped their horses into a gallop and closed in. The combination of noise and man-scent sent the herd thundering across the plain. Yelling at the top of his voice, each hunter came up behind a buffalo and shot arrows into its back between the hip bone and the last rib, downward into the vital organs. His bow was so powerful that arrows often buried themselves up to the feathers or passed completely through the victim. If the arrow failed to penetrate deeply, he might ride alongside, reach over to pull it out, and use it again. It was a matter of pride, not an effort to save arrows. A brave who put too many arrows into an animal became a laughingstock. When a buffalo fell, the hunters shouted "Yihoo! Yihoo!" in triumph.

A wounded bull might turn on its pursuers, lifting horse and rider off the ground on its horns. Horses, their bellies split open, raced about, trailing their intestines behind them. Or a horse might step into a prairie dog hole, breaking a leg and throwing its rider. If he was lucky, the rider rolled clear. If not, he fell under the pounding hooves. The artist George Catlin was both thrilled and horrified at seeing a surround. He wrote in his 1844 book, *North American Indians*:

> [The buffalo], becoming infuriated with deadly wounds in their sides, erected their shaggy manes over their blood-shot eyes and furiously plunged forwards at the sides of their assailants' horses, sometimes goring them to death at a lunge, and putting their dismounted riders to flight for their lives. Sometimes their dense crowd was opened, and the blinded horsemen, too intent on their prey amidst the cloud of dust, were hemmed and wedged in amidst the crowding beasts, over whose backs they were obliged to leap for security, leaving their horses to the fate that might await them in the results of this wild and desperate war. Many were the bulls that turned upon their assailants and met them with desperate resistance; and many warriors who were dismounted, and saved themselves by the superior muscles of their legs. Some who were closely pursued by the bulls, wheeled suddenly around and snatching the part of a buffalo robe from their waists, threw it over the horns and eyes of the infuriated beast and, darting by its side, drove the arrow or the lance into its heart. . . . I had sat in trembling silence upon my horse, and witnessed this extraordinary scene, which allowed not one of these animals to escape out of my sight.[11]

As many as three hundred buffalo could be killed in a surround lasting fewer than ten minutes.

✕   ✕   ✕

Comanche braves, like the men of all Plains tribes, were, above all, warriors. They hunted to live, but they lived to fight. War was their passion, at once a pleasure and a necessity, essential to their entire way of life.

Today, the idea of "pleasurable" war seems weird; twentieth-century Americans have had a bellyful of fighting in every corner of the globe. We see war as a calamity to be avoided at almost any cost. Yet The People's world was not ours, and they saw things differently. The idea that humans should always live in peace seems never to have entered their minds. It was war and not peace that was natural. They were constantly at war. They handed on their wars from generation to generation, like so many family heirlooms. They fought to protect their hunting grounds and to seize fresh ones. They fought for loot: horses to ride, women to enslave, children to adopt into the band. They fought to punish insults and, in "mourning wars," to avenge those killed in past conflicts.

Above all, they fought because the warpath was the path of honor. The People were hunters, and hunting means spilling blood. From his earliest days, a boy knew he was born to kill. A man who could not kill, or kill efficiently, could not survive in the harsh world of the Great Plains. Unable to feed his family, much less defend it, he was useless to everyone. A man was judged by his killing skill, strength, and courage. But courage was valued above all else, as it should have been; for without courage, every skill was meaningless. And since war was the ultimate test of courage, it was also the true measure of a man.

Brave deeds made one a "brave." They made a man proud of himself and brought him the respect of others. Nor was he shy about his accomplishments. He never missed an opportunity, which was often, to boast of his mighty deeds. Others sought him out, praised him, wanted to be known as his friend. However, anyone who had not proven himself in battle was not regarded as

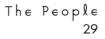

Stripped down and ready for action. A Plains warrior as seen by the artist Frederic Remington.

a man. Nobody respected him, admired him, asked his advice, or obeyed him. No woman would marry him until he earned the right in battle. Thus, there was a genuine horror of peace. A band at peace was an unhappy band. Bored and aimless, its men longed to gain honor in the only way they knew.

No knight ever went on a crusade better armed than a man of The People. His main attack weapon was the bow and arrow. Made of wood wrapped tightly with sinew for extra "spring," a bow was highly accurate at fifty yards; at fifteen yards it could drive an arrow clear through a buffalo—or a person. Hunting arrows had long, tapered points that could be pulled out easily. War arrows had barbed, swept-back points. It was impossible to pull them out without doing further damage; besides, they were loosely attached to the shaft so as to break off in the wound. Arrowheads were made of flint, bone, or iron. Iron was highly valued; white settlers might be attacked just for the iron hoops on their water buckets. White traders also sold machine-made arrowheads in packets of twelve; a buffalo robe bought one packet, a huge profit for the trader.

A skilled bowman, riding at full gallop, could keep eight arrows in the air at once. At close quarters, he used a fourteen-foot lance tipped with flint or iron and a club made of a round stone tied to a wooden handle. Tomahawks had flint blades; occasionally, iron-bladed tomahawks were obtained from traders.

Each brave carried a shield for defense. Shields were made of layers of tough hide from the shoulder of a buffalo bull. The space between the layers was filled with feathers and hair to absorb the force of any weapon. Paper, however, was the best filling. One captured shield contained a complete history of Rome; those who raided Fort Parker took Bibles for the same purpose. A new shield was set up as a target for arrows and bullets. If pierced at fifty yards, it was thrown away as useless. Old-fashioned musket balls could not penetrate a good shield unless they struck head-on. Shields were decorated with human scalps, bear claws, and horse tails to symbolize the owner's deeds as a warrior, skill as a hunter, and performance as a thief. Its rim was surrounded with eagle feathers, which fluttered at the slightest movement, throwing off the enemy's aim. When attacking, a brave held his shield in front. When retreating, he slung it over his back.

Anyone could be a war chief if he could convince others to follow him. A brave was a free person and could not be made to fight against his will. He was always a volunteer, joining a war party because he trusted its leader, a man of proven ability. Even if he went along, he was not bound to go on to the bitter end. He could turn back at any time, for any reason. If he lost faith in the leader, or began to feel unlucky, he left the war party. No one questioned his decision or thought him a coward.

A brave who wished to lead a war party rode through the village with an eagle-feather banner on a lance. Anyone who wanted to join fell in behind him. Day after day, he and his followers paraded, dancing, singing, and gathering volunteers until the war party was strong enough. If the war chief was an exceptional leader, messengers would be sent to other bands for recruits. Warriors provided their own equipment, particularly horses. Each brought at least two mounts, and sometimes as many as five. These were no ordinary buffalo horses, but animals trained and used only for war. A favorite mount, chosen for its endurance and calmness, was ridden only in battle; the others served as spares.

War parties set out at night. Legend had it that a war party once left in daylight; no one returned, and from then on warriors only left after dark. As they rode away, they serenaded their wives and sweethearts. A favorite song would have touched the heart of any twentieth-century American soldier:

> Going away tonight;
>   Be gone a long time.
> While I'm gone,
>   I'll be thinking of you.[12]

Comanche horse thieves as painted by Charles M. Russell. Whites hung horse thieves, because, in stealing a man's only transportation, the thief was actually sentencing him to a slow death on the vast plains. The Comanche, however, regarded a skillful horse thief as a hero, because he went deep into enemy territory, risking his life to prove his courage.

A long time meant just that: some war parties were away two years.

On the war trail, the chief was in total control. He set the objective, appointed the scouts, chose the route, and planned the attack. The responsibility lay heavily on his shoulders; Comanche lives were precious, and he must not risk them needlessly. Everyone understood that courage was not the same as going out of your way to get hurt. That is stupidity. No leader would accept battle on equal terms if he could avoid it. Nor would he order an attack knowing that even one of his men would surely die.

The best attack was a surprise attack, since it took the enemy off guard and minimized casualties. And there was no shame in retreating if things went wrong. A live warrior could fight another day, a dead one was lost to The People forever. Braves were amazed that whites should hold their ground, or charge a waiting enemy, against all odds. Even more amazing was that generals who had lost many men should be hailed as heroes. The People saw them as fools and criminals.

Comanche tactics were simple—and deadly. There were no night assaults, because of fear that being killed in the dark could cause the souls to wander, lost and alone, throughout eternity. A war party approached a target in the moonlight, all but invisible on the Plains. The hours before dawn were used to prepare for battle. A brave dressed for battle by taking his clothes off, not putting them on. Clothes meant more weight for his horse to carry, tiring it more easily. Besides, an arrow or bullet could drive a piece of clothing into a wound, causing infection.

Paint replaced clothing. The People, both men and women, loved to paint their faces and bodies. Paint applied every morning protected against sunburn and the buffalo gnat, a tiny terror with a bite like an electric needle. Each person used their favorite colors—reds, blues, yellows, browns, greens—in their favorite patterns of stripes, circles, dots, and zigzags. Such designs were not meant to frighten anyone, but to be exciting and beautiful. War paint, however, gave the brave a fiendish appearance. Coal black, the death color, it was daubed in stripes across the face and forehead.

A Texan named John Holland Jenkins described a war party in its full regalia. "It was a spectacle never to be forgotten, the wild, fantastic band as they stood in battle array," he wrote in the 1830s. "Both horses and riders were decorated most profusely, with all the beauty and horror of their wild taste combined. Red Ribbons streamed out of their horses' tails as they swept around us, riding fast. . . . There was a huge warrior, who wore a stovepipe hat, and another who wore a fine pigeon-tailed cloth coat, buttoned up behind. Some wore on their heads immense buck and buffalo horns. . . . They . . . exhibit feats of horseman-ship and daring none but a Comanche . . . could perform."[13]

Raiders struck from the east, charging with the rising sun at their backs. Their victims, groggy with sleep and blinded by the sun's glare, were quickly overrun. But if surprise was not possi-ble, the Comanche had to fight an alert enemy in the open.

Now the aim was to present the smallest target possible, and that a quickly moving one. Warriors never bunched up, but advanced in a V-formation until they came within striking range. Then the two "wings" separated and began circling the enemy to the right and left. It was like a buffalo surround, only the prey was human—and it shot back. Using his horse as a shield, each brave rode in close, dropped into the loop woven into his horse's mane, and shot his arrows. If his mount went down, a comrade snatched him from the ground, carrying him out of danger on his horse. If the enemy charged, he broke off the attack, reformed, and swept in from the flank. An enemy who panicked was a goner. The worst thing you could do was turn your back on a Comanche. When that happened, he sped forward with a stream of arrows or a lance.

A fallen enemy was in deep trouble. Religion was the reason. Indians believed that the dead went to the Happy Hunting Ground. They went there not as a reward for living a good life, as with the Christian heaven, but as a continuation of their lives on earth. The only difference was that life was easier, since game was plentiful and the climate mild. They stayed there forever, warm in winter, their bellies full, without sadness or pain. If, however, they fell into enemy hands before death, the future was bleak.

The first warrior to touch a fallen victim cried *"A-he!"* ("I claim it!") at the top of his voice. What he claimed was the victim's scalp. It has sometimes been said that whites introduced Indians to scalping. This is not so. Whites did pay bounties for enemy scalps, as in the French and Indian War, 1756–1763. Nevertheless, Indians had been scalping each other for centuries before whites arrived in the New World.

Scalping was tied in with certain religious ideas. It was believed that hair is an extension of a person's spirit, or soul. Whoever owned the hair also controlled the spirit. Living persons wore their own hair. They spent hours each day combing it and greasing it with buffalo fat. And the longer the hair, the better; hair was only cut when mourning the loss of a loved one. In battle, however, a brave would grab his victim's hair with one hand and cut around the scalp with a knife. A quick jerk brought it away from the skull in one piece. Scalping did not necessarily bring death; scalping victims could (and did) survive, without endangering their souls. But to kill a person and then scalp him destroyed his soul, so there was no part of the brave to enter the afterlife.

Mutilating the dead without scalping was the worst thing imaginable. The belief was that you entered the next world as you were at the time of death, and stayed that way. Thus, someone with a toothache had it forever, and a cripple remained crippled. Those killed in warfare might be hacked to bits, slashed, and their limbs cut off for the same reason. If their souls were not destroyed by scalping, they spent eternity in agony. The need to prevent scalping and mutilation explains why warriors risked their lives to keep fallen comrades out of enemy hands. Indian warfare was forever.

Once battle was joined, a brave neither expected mercy nor

showed it. Unless knocked unconscious or overpowered by superior numbers, he never allowed himself to be taken alive. If escape was impossible, he took off his moccasins as a sign of his vow to fight to the death. At the last moment, when all was hopeless, he sang his death song. This song, composed before his first raid and constantly practiced, helped him stay in control to the end. If he was killed, he died with dignity. If he was captured, he needed to be calm for the ordeal ahead. A captured brave was always tortured to death.

Whites, as we shall see, committed suicide rather than face torture. A brave never took his own life. He knew what to expect, and that he must face it as a self-respecting man.

Indians were not alone in the use of torture. The practice was widespread among "civilized" whites until the late 1700s as a punishment, as a means of gaining evidence in court trials, and to obtain confessions. European governments hired experts, who knew human anatomy so well that they could cause excruciating pain while keeping the victim alive for days. Using torture for such reasons was unthinkable to the Native American, since it deprived the victim of any shred of self-respect. The brave owed that much even to a hated enemy.

Torture was meant to be a test of wills, the supreme test of courage. The brave was not supposed to give in to pain. Whatever happened, he must not cringe, cry, whimper, scream, or beg. The greater his courage, the more he proved his manhood and superiority to his enemy. Only one man, and a white at that, is on record as surviving capture by The People. We know nothing about him, except that he had exceptional courage. When faced with torture, he stood tall and laughed in his captors' faces. He was so convincing that the war chief patted him on the back, saying "bravo!" He was adopted into the band, but stole a horse and escaped.[14]

Sooner or later, the war party returned to its band. A successful party galloped into the village whooping and boasting of its deeds. That night was given to dancing and feasting. If only loot was taken, they held a Victory Dance; if they had scalps it was a Scalp Dance, or "Hair-Kill Dance." The scalps were attached to a tall pole set up at the center of the dance circle, near a blazing fire. Men, women, and children danced and celebrated until dawn. The Great Spirit had smiled upon them. It was good to be alive.

But if braves had been lost, the war party slipped into the village unannounced. Entering a few at a time, its members quietly went to their tipis. The war chief, however, had a lot of explaining to do. How did his men die? Could their deaths have been avoided? Were they secretly buried to prevent scalping or mutilation? Why were their bodies abandoned? The questions came thick and fast, and he had to answer truthfully. If he was at fault, he lost all respect and no one ever trusted him again.

Meantime, the families of the fallen went into mourning. Men unbraided their hair and cut deep gashes into their legs. Women's mourning was something dreadful. At the loss of a male relative, they tore off their clothing and hacked off their hair. Most slashed their breasts, faces, arms, and legs with sharp flints. Some cut off one or more fingers, or even an ear, moaning and howling for days thereafter.

Comanches always seemed to be in mourning, which called for yet another mourning war.

✖   ✖   ✖

When The People first reached the High Plains, they found them occupied by other Indians. Among them was a tribe that claimed the lands stretching eastward from the Pueblo country to the Plains. The Zuni, a branch of the Pueblo Indians, called them *ápachu* (Apache), or "enemies." They called themselves *Tindé*, "People Superior to All Others." Whatever the name, those who met them found them to be fierce warriors.

The Apache had long been enemies of Spain. The trouble began with horse stealing and steadily escalated in violence.

Apache horse raids were avenged by Spanish slave raids. Batches of Apache men, women, and children were tied together and marched deep into Mexico. The men were sold to mine owners. Women and children became household servants; attractive girls were forced into prostitution.[15] But terror only produced more terror, as it always does. Captured Spaniards were tortured in gruesome ways, like being tied naked to giant cactus plants or hung head down over a cliff edge by one leg. It was enough to make strong men tremble. For over a century whites would rather be killed outright than undergo the cactus ordeal. It used to be said of bright youngsters: "He will make a fine man if the Apaches do not tie him to a cactus."[16]

The Apache met their match in the Comanche. It was like bringing together fire and gunpowder. The moment they touched, warfare exploded between them. The hard-riding Comanche had no trouble locating their foes and striking them at will. After all, they were nomads, seldom staying in a place for more than a few weeks. But the Apache were mainly farmers, hunting buffalo for only a short time each year. In a war of extermination, the Comanche attacked their villages, burning crops and massacring the inhabitants. Slowly but surely, they drove the Apache off the Plains, into the mountains and deserts of New Mexico. Yet that was just the beginning.

During the early 1700s, Spanish colonists crossed the Rio Grande south of New Mexico. Moving eastward, they built their main settlement, San Antonio, in 1718. The first Indians they met were peaceful farmers called the Hasinai. Asked their name, the Hasinai spread their arms and cried "*tejas*," from their word for "friends." The Spanish thought it the name of their country, which they pronounced *teychas* or *tehas*. We know it as Texas.

The Texas colony grew slowly. In 1757, Spanish priests built a mission on the Rio San Saba, a branch of the Colorado River. Apaches living in the area had invited the *padres* (fathers) to teach them about Christianity. Becoming Christians, however, was the furthest thing from their minds. They knew that frontier missions were defended by *presidios*, forts manned by soldiers. The desperate Apache wanted a safe place to plant their crops and, if possible, turn the Spanish against their enemies. Until then, the Spanish had had little contact with The People.

The following year, the Apache would not go anywhere near the San Saba mission. They knew something was about to happen, and were keeping it to themselves. Sure enough, in March 1758 two thousand Comanches came looking for trouble. Thinking the Spanish had allied themselves with the Apache, they meant to teach the whites a lesson. And what a lesson it was! They killed as many Spaniards as they could put their hands on and burned the mission to the ground; the survivors took refuge in the *presidio*. Now the Spaniards had two stubborn enemies. After Mexico won its independence in 1821, both tribes continued to fight the new nation, while continuing to fight each other.

No Mexican was safe anywhere. In Texas, Comanche and Apache raiders made every journey a life-threatening ordeal. Travelers were waylaid and wagon trains attacked. No Spanish soldier ventured north or west of San Antonio for fear of an ambush. Not even that town was safe. In 1825, for example, Comanches occupied San Antonio for six days. They entered private homes, taking whatever they wished, including several scalps.

The heaviest blows fell on Mexico itself. Mexicans dreaded the "Comanche Moon," the full moon of summer, when horsemen with black stripes painted on their faces rode "The Great Comanche War Trail." Stretching a thousand miles, the trail began north of the Red River, ran east of the Staked Plain, and struck the Rio Grande at a shallow spot called "The Grand Indian Crossing." It was impossible to miss the trail, noted John Love, an American army officer and explorer. "It is very wide, well beaten, and resembles a much traveled thoroughfare" that could be seen clearly from the mountains. The raiders often traveled in parties of six to eight hundred warriors.[17]

Splashing across the Rio Grande, they spread out across the Mexican states of Chihuahua and Coahuila. "*Los bárbaros! Los*

bárbaros!" The alarm went from farmhouse to farmhouse, ranch to ranch, town to town. "The barbarians are coming! The barbarians are coming!" Wherever Comanches went, they traced a path of fire and blood across the land. *Paisanos* (townspeople) were slaughtered and *ranchos* (ranches) left in ashes. Horses and mules were stolen in droves. Driven hard, countless animals died, their bones littering the trail for hundreds of miles on both sides of the Rio Grande.

Mexico was gripped by the Comanche terror. Even when they outnumbered the raiders, citizens might be too frightened to act. One day, for example, a lone Comanche galloped into the public square of Durango, five hundred miles north of Mexico City. Though Durango had thirty thousand inhabitants, none dared face him. Instead, they shuttered their shops and locked themselves in their homes, praying to be spared from this "scourge of God." The warrior stayed an hour, exploring the empty streets at his leisure. He was only captured when someone lassoed him from a window as he rode out of town. "The sight of a half-naked Comanche," wrote an American visitor, "with his shaggy horse and his quiver of arrows produces a paralysis of fear from which he [the Mexican] seems never to recover. These wretched people will look forth despairingly but without even an inclination to resist, upon . . . Comanches ravaging the fields and *haciendas* under their eyes, and carrying off into hopeless captivity the miserable women and children who have not succeeded in making good their escape."[18]

The Mexican army was little help against such a foe. The Comanche always chose when and where to strike. By the time the army learned of a raid, the attackers had made their getaway. Pursuit, even by cavalry, was hopeless. The war party simply broke into small groups, each going a separate way and reuniting at an agreed spot. Masters at hiding their trail, braves rode over rocky ground, crossed and recrossed streams, and traveled over prairies where the short grass sprang back as they passed. Even if the cavalry found a trail, they seldom caught the raiders. Whenever a brave's horse tired, he leaped onto the back of a spare mount without breaking stride. In this way he might cover a hundred miles by sundown.

The Mexican government hired bounty hunters to bring in Comanche and Apache scalps. An adult male's scalp was worth two hundred gold pesos, the scalps of women and children half as much. Both Mexicans and Americans took part in this dirty business. Bounty hunters lured Indians into villages with promises of gifts, then shot them from ambush or fed them poisoned food. The Indians were shocked at such dishonorable conduct. They obeyed the law of hospitality by which any visitor, including an enemy, must be helped if he asked for food and a place to sleep. Worse, since it was impossible to tell a "wild" from a "tame" Indian's hair—or from a Mexican's for that matter—hundreds of innocent people were killed and their scalps sold to government agents. But the raiders kept coming.

By the early 1800s, The People ruled the *Comanchería* ("The Land of the Comanche"), an empire teeming with buffalo and other game. Stretching from the Arkansas River in the north to the Rio Grande in the south, it included parts of the future states of Texas, Oklahoma, Kansas, Colorado, and New Mexico. The Comanche shared this country with the Kiowa, the "First" or "Principal People." A small tribe, the Kiowa were worthy allies. Kiowa raiders stabbed deeper into Mexico than even the

Comanche. One war party went as far as Guatemala, returning with tales of monkeys and parrots. Man for man, the Kiowa were also the deadliest warriors of all, killing more whites in proportion to their numbers than any other tribe. And most of their victims were Texans.

Soon after becoming independent, Mexico invited "Anglos," Americans of British descent, to settle in Texas. Since few Mexicans wished to move to Texas, the government had decided that an Anglo colony would form a human barrier between the Comanche and the Mexican border. The newcomers would support their adopted homeland not only against *Los bárbaros*, but also against the United States. After President Thomas Jefferson purchased the Louisiana Territory from France in 1803, Mexicans feared American expansion. An Anglo colony seemed the best way to keep restless Americans out of the Southwest.

Settlers poured into Texas, attracted by offerings of free land. At first, all went well; their settlements lay outside the *Comanchería* and they had little contact with its inhabitants. Yet there were those who knew the Comanche could not be taken lightly. Colonel Edward Stiff of the United States Army visited several Comanche bands in the 1830s. He found them to be "kind, open and liberal to strangers, and at once brave and generous to a fault." But, he warned, "were this tribe provoked to hostilities, or induced to believe that peace was not for their interest or honor, the present population of Texas would be exterminated and their homes made desolate in a brief space of time. So, ye wise ones, beware."[19]

The tragedy was that Comanche and Anglo, Indian and white, could never see each other as fully human, with rights and feelings like themselves. Both had different ways of life and lived in different mental worlds. So different were they that few, if any, understood the other, much less sympathized with them.

The Comanche saw themselves as a part of nature. Nature, to them, simply existed, fixed and unchangeable, as the Great Spirit created it at the beginning of time. People, to live, must live within nature's limitations. They must treat it kindly, lovingly, giving thanks for everything they took. If they killed a buffalo, they must offer its spirit tobacco smoke in gratitude for allowing its flesh to be eaten. Before chopping down a tree, they must apologize to the tree's spirit and explain why they needed its wood. The Comanche, therefore, needed only an open country and enough game for food, clothing, and shelter. The land belonged to the Great Spirit's children, be they human or animal. The idea that a person could own the land seemed as ridiculous as claiming the sky and the stars.

Whites saw nature differently. God, they believed, had given man the world for his very own, to remake according to his needs and desires. "Wilderness" was an affront, something untamed and beyond human control. It had to be remade, broken as a brave broke a horse. This meant chopping down forests, plowing fields, damming streams, digging minerals from the earth, and annihilating "useless" creatures. It meant carving up the land into parcels, each owned by an individual or a family. Whites also saw the Indians as part of wild nature. The Indian, in their view, was an "inferior" being without laws, religion, government, morality, honor, and decency. If the Indian could not be "improved," he must be eliminated.

Each people, therefore, lacked understanding of the other's strengths and weaknesses. And where understanding is absent, conflict is inevitable.

By the mid-1830s, the settlements were advancing toward the Comanche hunting grounds. Fort Parker was closer than any previous Anglos had ever come. What Elder John saw as a good place to farm, the buffalo hunters saw as a threat and a challenge. The result was the events of May 19, 1836.

On that day the real struggle for the Southwest began. It would be the longest and bloodiest of any of the wars between whites and Indians. Soon—too soon—blows would be struck that neither side could forgive nor forget. It would be a war to the death, a war in which there could be only one winner.

Becoming a Comanche

"Miss Parker . . . has married an Indian Chief and is . . . wedded to the Indian mode of life."

—*Houston Telegraph and Texas Register*, June 1, 1846

THE Fort Parker raiders headed north, each captive tied securely behind a brave. For these five women and children, the journey was a nightmare become reality.

Thanks to Rachel Plummer, we know what the captives experienced and how it felt. After being held for nearly two years, she was returned to her relatives in Texas. Broken in body and spirit, she described her ordeal in a sad little book, *Rachel Plummer's Narrative, or Twenty-Two Months Servitude as a Prisoner Among the Comanche Indians*. She may have written it herself; most likely, she dictated it to another person. The book was to have a long life of its own. First printed in 1839, it became a classic in western "captivity literature" and was reprinted many times, even in the twentieth century, the last time in 1977.

Rachel describes a terrifying ride into the unknown. The captives were in a state of shock. The sights of Fort Parker were still before their eyes, its sounds still ringing in their ears. The women had seen relatives scalped and mutilated. The children probably had not, but knew that strangers—and *what* strangers!—were holding them against their will. The strangers traveled at top speed to outrun any pursuers. There was no stopping for food or rest, only to change horses and drink from buffalo-gut canteens. The greasy water made them gag, but at least it eased their thirst.

About midnight, they halted on the prairie, after fifteen hours in the saddle. Braves made camp, built a low fire, and threw their prisoners on the ground. A scalp dance followed. Rachel recalled:

> They now tied a plaited thong around my arms, and drew my hands behind me; they tied the thongs so tightly round my arms that the marks of them are to this day plainly to be seen. They then tied a similar thong round my ankles, and drew my feet and hands together, beating me over the head with their bows; they now turned me on my face, and I was unable to turn over, and it was with great difficulty that I could keep from smothering in my own blood, for the wound they gave me with the hoe, and many others, was bleeding freely. I could hear my little James Pratt crying for mother, and I could easily hear the blows they gave him, and sometimes his feeble voice was weakened by the blows. . . . Such horrid, undescribable yelling . . . while dancing around the scalps; kicking and sometimes stomping the prisoners. . . . They never allowed the prisoners to speak to one another.[1]

Thousands of Indian and Mexican captives had undergone a similar ordeal. Such treatment was normal during the early stages of captivity. On the one hand, it satisfied the warriors' lust for revenge; helpless captives, even babies, might be cut to pieces in anger. On the other hand, brutality served a useful purpose. It produced fear, and fear was power, enabling the raiders to gain total control of their captives. One dared not make a false move, let alone try to escape, for fear of the consequences.

Brutality was also a way of testing a youngster's strength and courage. Infants seldom survived the hardships of the trail, or were killed if they cried; the Comanche, as noted, left behind their own weak and aged if they became a burden. Older boys might be made to fight each other, supposedly to the death, to see how they behaved. Or they were tied to stakes and threatened with torture. Screaming warriors ran up to them waving knives, hatchets, and flaming torches. Sometimes they were tied to the back of an unbroken mustang or a buffalo calf, which was sent racing across the Plains. Cowards were killed in disgust.

Though Rachel does not mention it, the prisoners must have been stripped of practically all their clothing. Comanches rode the war trail nearly naked and they expected the same of their prisoners. Again, it was a practical matter. White women wore long, heavy dresses, which were fine in a settlement or for riding in a buggy. But in galloping across the Plains, all that cloth got in the way. Riding unprotected under the blistering sun, however, caused severe sunburn, a common complaint of other freed captives who told of their experiences. Sunburn on top of sunburn, day after day, tormented captives more than any beating.

On the fifth day (May 23, 1836), they crossed the Red River. The raiders, feeling safe at last, relaxed. The prisoners were untied and fed strips of dried buffalo meat. It was to be their last meal together. The war party broke up that afternoon, each group riding off with a captive in a different direction.

Elizabeth Kellogg was lucky; after six months, she was bought by Delawares for $150 worth of trade goods. The Delaware and other eastern tribes had been driven from their homes during the 1820s. Forced to walk the "Trail of Tears," on which hundreds starved and froze, they settled on reservations in the Indian Territory, the future state of Oklahoma. Victims themselves, they had sympathy for other victims, both red and white. They brought Elizabeth to General Sam Houston, asking in return only what they had spent.

Rachel Plummer was taken across the High Plains to eastern Colorado. After reaching the raiders' village, she became the slave of a warrior named Tall-as-the-Sky. She was his property, and he could do with her as he pleased. He could use her to pay off a gambling debt or sell her to another warrior for a fixed time. He could also, and probably did, sexually abuse her. Women captives were usually raped. Colonel Richard Irving Dodge of the United States Army was an experienced plainsman. In the 1870s, he noted that "no woman has, in the last thirty years, been taken prisoner by any wild Indians who did not . . . become a victim to the brutality of every one of . . . her captors." The word "brutality," as used here, was a polite term for rape.[2]

Tall-as-the-Sky's wife set Rachel to work. Nothing could satisfy that slave driver. It was a happy day indeed when she did not beat Rachel until the blood came. One day, however, she went too far. She was raising her stick when Rachel twisted it out of her hand and gave her a taste of her own medicine. Villagers came running when they heard the uproar. But instead of killing Rachel, as she expected, they patted her on the shoulder and said *"Bueno! bueno!"*—"Good! good!" From then on, they called her Fighting Squaw and treated her better. She had proven her courage in a way The People admired.[3]

Rachel was seen by some Comancheros, Mexican-born traders who made regular visits to the *Comanchería*. Every spring they set out from Santa Fe, New Mexico, across the Staked Plain. Their carts were loaded with things The People wanted: brightly colored cloth, paint, mirrors, beads, knives, hatchets, guns, ammunition, sugar, coffee. In exchange, they took buffalo robes, stolen horses, and anything else they might be able to resell at a profit. They also dealt in Mexican and Anglo captives. War parties often met in Quitaque Canyon to swap captives; it was a place of so much misery that it became known as the *Valle de las Lágrimas*, or "Valley of Tears."

The Comancheros were coldhearted businessmen. Captives were bought from the Comanche for resale to their families. If they could not locate the families, or if the families could not afford to pay what they demanded, the captives were traded to other Comanche bands or murdered. Comancheros bought

Rachel Plummer, then resold her to an American merchant in Santa Fe at a good profit. He returned her to her family. She never got over the ordeal. It preyed on her mind, slowly destroying her will to live. She ended her book with this pitiful cry: "Where is my poor little James Pratt!" She died on February 19, 1839.[4]

James Pratt Plummer was ransomed in 1842. By then, his skin was dark from years of exposure to sun and wind. He spoke no English, but quickly relearned his native language. John Parker was ransomed at about the same time. Now twelve, he, too, readjusted to life among the whites. His mother later sent him back to the High Plains to find his sister, Cynthia Ann. He never did. During the Civil War, he served in the Confederate army. After the war, he married a Mexican woman and settled on a ranch near the Rio Grande.

Cynthia Ann became a Comanche. We cannot be sure how this happened, or what she thought of it at the time. Except for the first week of her captivity, described so vividly by Rachel Plummer, she was lost to history for a quarter of a century. Indians, we recall, had no written language and kept no records of events other than those passed on by word of mouth. We do not know, and can never know, the details of how this white girl grew into a woman of The People. Still, it is not a total mystery. Her experiences could not have been very different from those of other "white Indians." And here we have plenty of information: the recollections of freed captives, reports by white travelers, interviews with Comanche women on the reservation. Based on these, we can reconstruct, in outline, Cynthia Ann's life as a captive.

She had been taken by the Nokoni Comanche, who at that time were camped near the Wichita Mountains in the Indian Territory. When the war party returned, she would have been placed with a family, probably one that had recently lost a daughter. Then, or very soon thereafter, she was renamed; from then on, Cynthia Ann would be known as Naduah. The woman of the family became her guardian, instructing her in the ways of The People.

There was a lot to learn and get used to. Naduah had entered a strange world, a world as different from the one she had left as day is from night.

The bustling camp echoed to the noises of work and play. Women, some carrying somber-faced babies in cradleboards on their backs, worked and gossiped at the top of their voices. Warriors stood around in groups, bragging of their adventures, or sat quietly by themselves, smoking their pipes. Gangs of naked little boys laughed and shouted and ran about freely. Others, boys as well as girls, sat around a fire, listening to a storyteller's tales. Whinnying horses competed with packs of barking dogs.

Strong, offensive odors filled the air. Plains Indians did not believe that cleanliness is next to godliness. Sanitation was nonexistent. Horse manure littered the ground, attracting swarms of blue- and green-tailed flies. Food wastes were not collected, but thrown around the campsite to rot. Soap was unknown; even if it had been, The People seldom used water for anything other than drinking. "In their habits they are supremely nasty," recalled Nelson Lee, a white boy who escaped after three years in captivity. "Occasionally, in warm weather, they bathe in the river, but daily ablutions are not thought of, so that they are constantly covered with dirt and vermin." Body lice might be eaten as "a dainty," according to another captive.[5]

Naduah lived in a tipi, or lodge, a cone-shaped tent of buffalo skins supported on a framework of wooden poles. These were driven diagonally into the ground in a circle and an opening left at the top for smoke to escape. The tipi was from twelve to fifteen feet in diameter and fifteen feet high. An all-weather home, its shape kept it from being overturned by high winds. In summer, the skins were rolled up a few inches above the ground, allowing the air to circulate; in winter, an extra lining was added for warmth. A small fire of buffalo chips kept the tipi cozy even on the coldest days.

For anyone used to living in a stone house, or even a log cabin, the tipi was cramped. Its single room served for cooking,

Opposite page: A band of Plains Indians camped near a stream. While the men were out hunting buffalo, the extra horses were watered. Plains tribes were nomadic, moving from place to place in pursuit of the buffalo herds.

eating, sleeping, receiving guests, and storing all the family's possessions except the horses. Beds were piles of buffalo robes arranged along the tipi's sides, pillows the skins of small animals stuffed with straw. A dozen people, plus any number of dogs, might live in this small space. Yet, despite the noise and crowding, they never seemed to get in each other's way. Privacy was impossible, and this bred a lack of modesty. The People were not shy about their bodies, something that would have made Naduah uncomfortable at first; proper white folks never let children go around naked, let alone do so themselves. Comanche youngsters did not have to be told the facts of life.

The camp may have seemed disorderly to Naduah, but it was really well run. Not that there were any formal rules. The People had no government or laws as whites understood these terms. Each band had a peace chief, or headman, who was a renowned hunter and warrior. Admired for his courage and wisdom, he was simply recognized as the leader. "No one made him such; he just got that way," a Comanche explained.[6] Yet he could not give orders. He merely offered suggestions, which others accepted or rejected as they wished. When important matters were to be decided, the chief and other respected men met in council. After discussing the issue from every angle, the council decided, usually by a unanimous vote. These discussions might last for days, and would have done credit to any congress or parliament. No one ever interrupted a speaker, or raised his voice, or used harsh words in council. Everyone acted with great dignity and consideration for the feelings of its members.

Naduah learned that, although cruel to outsiders, The People were gentle and considerate toward one another. A Texas lawman named Noah Smithwick had visited another band shortly before her capture. It was nothing like he'd imagined. "I never saw a woman or child abused," he recalled. "An Indian brave would have felt it a burning disgrace to strike a woman. Taking them all around, they were the most peaceable community I ever lived in."[7] That made a lot of sense. In their wanderings, nomads met strangers as competitors and enemies. With a need to cooperate for hunting and defense, small bands could not afford to feud among themselves. Thus, a Comanche was safer in a camp filled with fierce warriors than a citizen of any frontier town or, for that matter, any twentieth-century American city.

Naduah's tipi had no locks, no bars, no gates. The Comanche trusted each other, and assumed everyone would act properly if properly taught. Tipis were left open and unguarded. Valuables were left lying around. If an article was lost, the camp crier announced when it had been found and where to claim it. Stealing from outsiders, and not being caught, was honorable. But stealing from a fellow Comanche was disgraceful—and unnecessary. Generosity was such a virtue that anyone who wanted something only needed to ask for it. A thief was given just one chance to mend his ways. The first offense brought a public whipping, not so much to inflict pain, but as a humiliation and a warning. One repeat offender, whose eyes were put out, never stole again. Rough justice, to be sure, but it worked.

Murder was almost unheard of among the Comanche. But when it happened, the rule was "an eye for an eye and a tooth for a tooth." The victim's family hunted down the murderer and killed him. The murderer's own family stood by, keeping out of the quarrel and never trying to avenge his death. This avoided a "blood feud" in which each killing provoked another, until both families were annihilated.

Private quarrels that threatened band unity were not tolerated. When, for example, one brave took a dislike to and bullied another, the council stepped it. The aggressor was stripped naked, tied faceup on the ground, and left in the broiling sun for a day. "At night they loosed him and made us sleep together. He never tried to harm me anymore."[8] Another time, the council invited the band to gather in a circle around two quarrelsome braves. In the arena formed, the enemies' left arms were tied together with strips of rawhide. Each was given a knife in his right hand and, at the chief's signal, they went at each other.

Blades flashed. Blood spurted. Both fell dead. Had one brave survived, his own brother would have had to cut his throat. The welfare of the band, not the individual, always came first.

Captives were put to work by their guardians. Boys tended horses, a vital job among bands with such large herds. Girls were given necessary tasks that required little skill: chopping wood, gathering berries, tidying up the tipi. If they did well, after a year or so they would be adopted by their guardian's family. The Comanche, like all Plains tribes, were eager to adopt young captives. Disease and warfare took such a heavy toll that, to keep strong, they had to replace lost members with outsiders. It made no difference whether these were fellow Indians or whites, so long as they showed promise. Elsewhere, as in Florida, the Seminole adopted runaway slaves. In South America, escaped blacks, called Cimaroons, were adopted by jungle tribes.

Young children were especially welcome, because they were not yet set in their ways. Youngsters—and the younger the better—forgot faster and learned easier than adults. They forgot how they came to their adopted families. Memories of their capture and of their birth parents gradually faded. Surrounded by Comanche speakers, they soon forgot their own language; indeed, they *thought* in Comanche.

Adoption was a kind of second birth, at the end of which the child shed his or her white identity and became a Comanche in body, mind, and spirit. Everything was done to help them along the way. Adopted children were cherished members of the family, made to feel loved and needed. They became, a white noted, "the husbands of their daughters and the mothers of their children."[9] They hunted, fought, married, and had children as if they had been born into the band. Regardless of origin, they were judged purely on their merits. Adopted boys became war chiefs, showing no mercy to whites. Some Comanche camps held upward of three hundred adopted children. The Kiowa had more; in the 1890s, an estimated one-fourth of all the Kiowa had Mexican ancestors.[10]

Like her Comanche sisters, Naduah matured early. By the age of thirteen, she was considered a woman. She wore a buckskin dress and moccasins decorated with beads and bits of iron called "tinklers." Rings hammered from Mexican silver coins glistened on her fingers. As many as twenty bracelets of brass adorned her wrists; hoops of brass wire dangled from her pierced ears. She painted a red line in the part of hair, and greased the hair itself with buffalo fat. Red was a sacred color binding her to the earth, which bears its fruit in season, as she hoped to bear children. She loved to color the insides of her ears red, accent her eyes with red and yellow lines above and below the lids, and paint her cheeks with orange circles and triangles. She could, if she wished, also tattoo her breasts with various designs. Tattooing was popular with both women and men.

Naduah's mother taught her all she needed to know to be a wife, or "squaw." Main rule: daily tasks were strictly separated according to sex. There was no such thing as a man helping a woman with the housework. Men hunted, fought, and protected their families, as the Great Spirit intended. A squaw would not allow her husband to do anything for himself; serving him was a matter of her womanly pride. She saddled his horse when he left camp and unsaddled it when he returned. She made everything the family needed except weapons. When game became scarce, or the camp got too dirty, she did the moving. As soon as the chief gave the signal, she took down the tipi, which could be struck in three minutes and set up in five. She then put the tipi and the family's other belongings on a horse travois.

Strung out for miles across the Plains, a Comanche band was an impressive sight. "According to Indian custom," a European traveler wrote, "they rode single file, the men in advance, dressed in their best, looking about, dignified and grave; the lively squaws following, sitting astride like the men, each usually carrying a black-eyed little papoose on her back and another in front of the saddle. At the same time they kept a watchful eye on the pack horses which carried the [tipi] skins and the various household goods."[11]

The horse made it possible for Plains tribes to follow the wandering buffalo herds upon which they lived. The horse-drawn travois enabled them to transport everything, including young children, easily. Packing, loading, and unpacking were always woman's work.

Arriving at a new campsite, the squaw unpacked, set up the tipi, made the beds, brought wood and water, and cooked the next meal. There were no set hours for meals; you ate when you felt hungry. Breakfast was simply a long strip of meat propped up over a fire on the point of a stick, the other end thrust into the ground. Each family member cut off a piece and ate it half raw. Roasted prairie dogs, a captive recalled, were "exceedingly sweet, tender, and juicy," as were skunks. An unborn mustang boiled in its own juices was a special treat. Even more delicious was the flesh of a roasted dog or a tender, juicy puppy.[12] Buffalo, however, was the basic dish.

Naduah, at thirteen, would have taken part in the great buffalo hunts. Comanche girls learned to ride almost as soon as they could walk. They rode as well as any brave, except they could not

do war tricks on horseback. No matter; they followed the hunters, chasing animals that broke out of the surround with bows and arrows. Women were almost as skilled with this weapon as their menfolk, lacking only the strength to send an arrow clear through a buffalo.

The hunter and his family shared the kill. It was a feast, as joyful to them as the whites' Thanksgiving dinners. The buffalo's veins were opened and the blood drunk warm. A nursing cow's udder was slashed and the blood and milk lapped up, as was the curdled milk found in the belly of a calf. Everyone gnawed on chunks of meat or drew greasy guts between their fingers, squeezing out the half-digested green mush. Stomach, intestines, kidneys, and lungs were eaten as they were cut from the animal. They were eaten raw, since the Comanche liked the taste, and because building a fire on the open Plains might attract enemies. The hunter, of course, took the best parts for himself. He liked nothing better than to reach into a warm carcass up to the elbows with both arms. Sitting on his haunches, he then dragged the liver onto his lap and ate it spiced with the salty yellow ooze from the gall bladder.

The squaw butchered the rest of the buffalo. Its meat was wrapped in its own skin and taken back to camp on a horse travois. The tongue and hump ribs were barbecued over fires of buffalo chips. Other cuts of meat were made into stew. The animal itself provided the cooking pot. The paunch, or lining of the stomach, was thick and tough. It was suspended from four poles, meat and water added, and red-hot stones dropped in to bring it to a boil. After it had served its purpose, the paunch-pot itself was eaten.

Women also preserved meat for later use. Some was "jerked"; that is, cut into long, thin strips and hung on racks to dry in the wind. Pemmican, known to whites as "Indian bread," was a special treat. Stone mallets were used to pound jerky into fine shreds, together with dried berries and nuts. The mixture was then packed between layers of melted fat and stored in lengths of intestine, like sausage. Pemmican could keep for three to four years, a tasty, nutritious winter food.

Buffalo hides were made into robes, blankets, and tipi covers. Tanning was woman's work, as much a source of pride to her as the warrior's trophies. A hide was stretched on the ground, fur side down, and fastened with wooden pegs. Using "fleshers" of stone and bone, she scraped away the fat and muscle. When the hide was smooth, she applied a solution of buffalo brains and water for ten days. Keeping the hide moist, she constantly rubbed it and stretched it with her hands. When it became soft and pliable, she let it dry. If necessary, she removed the fur with a mixture of water and wood ash. Wet ashes produced lye, which made the hair fall off; whites mixed lye with hog fat to make soap.

Housework was only part of the woman's duty. She was also a fighter, as dangerous as any warrior. She, too, had been taught the value of courage, only hers was the courage of desperation. When a camp was attacked, and braves could not cover their escape, the women fought like wildcats. There was no choice, since they knew what fate awaited captives. Not that they minded if their men abused the women of other tribes. Squaws often went along with war parties just for the fun of seeing a fight. As the men battled, they cheered them on and sniped with their bows and arrows.

If scalps were taken, after the Hair-Kill Dance squaws preserved them on special hoops. A twig was bent into a circular hoop, then rawhide thongs were put through the scalp to fasten it to the edges. When it dried, the squaw lined it with red cloth or painted it various colors. Her man used scalps to decorate his horse and weapons. Displayed on a pole outside the tipi, they showed that a mighty warrior lived inside.

Prisoners might be handed over to squaws and young girls for torture. For a warrior, there was no honor, only shame, in dying at women's hands, even though when it came to inflicting pain, they outdid their menfolk by far. No indignity was spared the victim. They jabbed him with torches, passing the flames back and forth across his naked body. They scalped him, stabbed him, put hot coals into his open wounds. His bones were broken one at a time, fingers crushed, and nose, ears, and lips cut off. His eyes were spared, so he could see the torturers at work. When they finished with him, he was hardly recognizable as a man.

Every girl dreamed of marrying, and usually did so in her early teens. There were widows among The People, but no old maids; being a wife and a mother was the only career open to a woman.

Wives were purchased, not courted. If a brave was attracted to a girl, he did not approach her, much less tell her of his interest. Instead, he sent an uncle or a male friend to her parents with a gift of horses. After some polite talk, the parents were informed that the horses were a formal marriage proposal—as if they didn't know that already. By keeping the horses, they signaled their acceptance of the offer; releasing them was a clear rejection. The girl's family accepted on her behalf. She was told of the proposal and that it would be good to have that generous fellow in the family. Parents had the right to kill a daughter who refused to marry the man of their choice.[13] There was no public announcement, no religious ceremony, no fine speeches. The groom simply took his bride to his tipi and lowered the door flap.

Unless she married a fairly young man, the bride probably shared him with other squaws. Comanche men were polygamists; that is, they had several wives at the same time. Polygamy, The People believed, was an absolute necessity. In a world where hunting accidents were common, and war never ceased, there were never enough men to go around. Since men were the providers and protectors, a woman without a man could not survive. Polygamy allowed every woman to have a mate and a chance at motherhood, thus keeping the band strong. It also allowed a brave to care for a dead brother's family by marrying his wife. Sisters often married the same husband, for he was a known quantity. When a brave went away with a war party, his brother was expected to stay with his wife, so she would not be lonely.

Polygamy was also a matter of economic justice. A Comanche once asked a Texan: "Why you work so hard? Why you have only one wife? Why you not marry two—three—six women—have somebody to do your work? White man, he heap big fool!"[14] A squaw could have asked the same question of the Texan's wife. Women of both races worked hard. But while the white woman was on her own, the squaw shared the work with her husband's other wives. She might actually scold him, demanding to know why he did not get more wives so she would have less to do. A brave with two or three wives kept them and their children in his tipi. If he had more wives, they lived in separate tipis. They slept on buffalo robes with strings leading to their husband's bed. When he wanted a certain wife, he pulled on the string.

Naduah was a prize catch for any brave. Being white was a real advantage in winning a mate. Though buffalo hunting provided more food, allowing the bands to grow in size, it brought other problems. The nomadic way of life took a toll on unborn infants. Heavy work and constant riding caused frequent miscarriages. As a result, squaws seldom bore more than two children; a family of three was considered exceptionally lucky. Pioneer families, however, were huge by comparison. The reason, Comanches thought, was that white women were more fertile than squaws. It certainly seemed that way even to white visitors on the frontier. A traveler in Texas told of spending a night with a family that had twenty-five children. This, he noted, was "a praiseworthy effort to settle the southwestern wilds."[15]

Naduah was married by the time she turned fourteen. Her husband was Peta Nocona ("He Who Travels Alone and Returns"), a war chief in the Nokoni band. About the year 1845, she became a mother for the first time. Their son was called Quanah, meaning "Fragrance" or "Sweet Scent." In the years that followed, Naduah had another boy named Pecos ("Peanut") and a girl called Topsannah ("Prairie Flower"). Most likely, she had other children who did not survive.

Peta Nocona was as proud of his wife as she was of herself. They certainly had a right to be proud. A squaw's giving birth was as courageous an act as a warrior's charging headlong into the enemy. Both risked a painful death and an eternity of suffering. He might go into the afterlife horribly mutilated by the enemy. If she died with her baby unborn, it would never be born in the next world and must be carried, labor pains and all, forever.

Even if the birth went well, The People did not allow every newborn to live. Though they welcomed children, they had to be "normal." If an infant was deformed, diseased, or a weakling, it was left out on the Plains to starve. No wonder whites never reported seeing a retarded Comanche child. Nor, for that matter, did they see any twins. The birth of twins, especially girl twins, was considered unlucky and unnatural. One or both were always abandoned. The decision was made not by the mother, but by the midwife, a squaw who helped with the delivery.[16]

The year after Quanah's birth, 1846, the Nokoni were visited by white traders. Colonel Leonard Williams, their leader, had been a neighbor of the Parkers and knew all about Cynthia Ann. Somehow he learned that she was in that very camp. Williams's offer to ransom her was turned down with a warning that he'd better not raise the subject again. He was, however, allowed to meet her. He spoke of her friends and relatives, asking if she wished to send them a message. She just stared at the ground, not saying a word.

Naduah did speak to another trader, Victor M. Rose, in 1851. When Rose asked her to return with him, she said plenty. "I am happily wedded," she insisted. "I love my husband, who is good and kind, and my little ones, who, too, are his, and I cannot forsake them!"[17] Rose did not mention if she spoke in English; she had been with the Comanche for fifteen years and had almost certainly forgotten her native tongue. But since he knew Comanche, he surely recorded her feelings, if not her exact words.

All her ties were to the Comanche now, and she was

A Comanche village as seen by the American artist George Catlin. Girls dressed modestly in buckskin outfits, but young boys always went naked during the warm months.

determined to remain one of them. That determination gave rise to a Texas legend. Rose's story spread through the settlements, growing more imaginative with each telling. Naduah was portrayed as a Comanche princess who, alongside the mighty Peta Nocona, ruled an empire on the Great Plains. Others, however, could not bring themselves to believe that a white might *want* to live among "savages." They were wrong on both counts.

Meantime, Quanah grew up in the ways of The People. He had loving parents who knew how to make him feel wanted and safe. But not pampered. He lived in a dangerous world, and had to learn to cope with it even as an infant. Quanah was free to crawl about, to explore, to get hurt—and to learn from experience. Yet one freedom, normal to white children, was strictly forbidden. Comanche children could not cry, for that might alert prowling enemies. The moment he began to cry, Naduah would pick him up or nurse him. But if he continued, she covered his mouth with the palm of her hand or dripped water into his nostrils until he learned to be quiet.

Quanah's parents did not teach their children general principles of right and wrong. Like all Comanche parents, they taught them to see things in practical terms. An action was not "good," but useful; not "bad," but harmful. They never shouted at their son, much less hit him; you never struck a person unless you meant to do harm. If he misbehaved, they reasoned with him, showing by example that certain actions were praised by the community, others scorned. But if reasoning failed, particularly when he was younger, they frightened him with threats. Bed wetters, for example, were told they would be fed mice if they did not control themselves. Disobedient youngsters were threatened with Big Cannibal Owl, a mythical bird that ate naughty boys and girls at night. Sometimes, if there was an older sister, she was the disciplinarian. One girl dragged her younger brother into the tipi, put a rawhide rope around his neck, and promised to hang him if he misbehaved. "I was really scared," he recalled years later.[18] Older children were embarrassed in front of the entire camp, a punishment that usually did not have to be repeated.

According to custom, Quanah was allowed as much freedom as possible. He was not expected to do any work around camp and was always treated with special consideration. All boys were treated this way. For to be a boy was to live always in expectation of violent death. According to the saying: "He is going to be a warrior and he may die young in battle."[19]

As a young child, Quanah went naked most of the year. This was normal for Comanche boys; girls wore small versions of their mothers' dresses. At the age of eight or nine, he put on a breechclout, like his father's. First a string was tied around the waist. A piece of cloth or buckskin was then drawn under the string in front, passed between the legs, and drawn under the string in back, the loose ends forming flaps hanging front and rear. The breechclout was a comfortable outfit, easy to replace when it got dirty or wore out.

Quanah's teacher was his father, his schoolroom the Great Plains. Peta Nocona trained his son as a coach trains an athlete. The training was constant, thorough, and harsh. Horsemanship was basic; riding had to become automatic, since a hunter-warrior must concentrate on other things when he is in action. Quanah got used to horses, their smell and their motions, by sitting in front of his father whenever he went riding. Or he was tied to the back of a gentle horse, which an older child led in circles for an hour or so each day. By the age of five, he was expected to manage a horse by himself. His skills grew with the passing years. By age nine, he could leap from one galloping horse to another. He could use his horse as a shield, reach down to pick colored pebbles off the ground at a gallop, and sleep while riding. If he fell, he was laughed at by his friends and, horror of horrors, by the girls. By fourteen, his body was as tough as rawhide and flexible as a bow. Chances were he also had scars to show for his efforts. Scars, after all, were badges of honor, and every boy wanted them. Boys without scars often tattooed them into their skin with a bone needle and charcoal dust.

While still a toddler, Quanah received a miniature bow and arrows and was taught to use them. Little boys started small, with birds and bugs. They shot hummingbirds with headless arrows split in front; the birds were caught in the split, studied, and released. The same arrows were also used to bring down grasshoppers, whose hind legs were eaten as a treat. Boys caught butterflies with their hands, rubbing their wings on their chests to "borrow" their speed and grace. Not only did they shoot arrows at targets, they, too, became targets. They had to stand in front of archers with only a shield, warding off a hail of blunt-tipped arrows. Or they stood there without a shield, twisting and turning to avoid the arrows. These might not break the skin, but they raised nasty bumps and could take out an eye.

Most importantly Quanah learned to rely on his eyes. Like all fathers, Peta Nocona drummed this rule into his head: Everything has a meaning, study it carefully, and be patient. There were countless bits of information to learn, each vital to survival. An eagle's feather split a certain way must have come from the headdress of a warrior from a certain tribe. That pile of sand yonder was thrown up by playful young deer. Your horse's twitching ears when there were no horseflies around, or a wolf's off-key howling, meant something was wrong and you had better be on guard. Spiderwebs helped predict the weather. In dry weather they were thin and long and high, but if rain was coming they were low, short, and thick. Even dung told a story, if you knew how to "read" it. You could tell by its shape, firmness, and warmth the kind of animal that left it, what it had eaten, and how long ago it had passed. Barley found in horse manure was a sure sign that Texans had passed; corn kernels indicated horses from Mexico.

Having mastered these skills, Quanah joined the Nokoni hunters. His first big kill—a deer or a buffalo—became a turning point in his life. Now he was ready to "make medicine."

The People believed that everything in nature has a spirit or soul. You could pray to each spirit to use its power for your benefit. For example, you prayed to the coyote spirit for wisdom, to the deer spirit for speed, to the eagle spirit for keen eyesight, and to the rain spirit to fill the water holes. Better yet, you could find your own personal guardian spirit to lend you its magical power, or "medicine."

A boy (but not a girl) found his guardian spirit through a "vision quest." He had been preparing for that quest ever since childhood. When the time came, he went alone to some out-of-the-way spot, wearing just moccasins and a breechclout. Seating himself on a buffalo robe, he neither ate nor drank, but stayed awake four days and nights, praying for a vision. To help it come, he smoked tobacco or sumac leaves in a bone pipe. The combination of hunger and fatigue, prayer and smoke, eventually brought a vision.

It could be anything: a snake slithering under a rock, a coyote howling, a mouse running, the rumble of distant thunder, grass waving in the breeze. The vision-spirit became his guardian and teacher. It gave him special songs to protect him and bring him success. It told him what places were bad luck and what foods to avoid. One brave, for instance, could not sleep with his head facing north; another should not drink from a cup while standing. Finally, it taught him to make a medicine bundle, his very own package of magical objects: bear claws, skunk tails, colored pebbles, horse hairs, or perhaps a dried raven. From that day on, he would not do anything important without making a fresh medicine bundle and asking the spirit's blessing.

Visions were as real to the Comanche as something we desire is real to us when we see it in a dream. We will never know what would have happened had a brave not made medicine on a given day, or ignored the spirit's warnings. What we do know is that belief in spirit helpers, like belief in God, might give him the extra confidence to win against heavy odds. The feeling that his medicine was weak could just as easily make him give up trying. Braves often left war parties if their guardian spirit sent a bad sign. Entire war parties fled in panic if, say, clouds suddenly blackened the sky. If the spirits were against you, nothing could bring success. There was no point even trying.

Those with very strong medicine became "medicine men." A medicine man was both a priest and a physician. As a priest, he used his magic to benefit the tribe as a whole. As a physician, he treated the sick. Wounds were different from sickness. Wounds had an obvious cause and could be treated by anyone who knew how. Every Comanche boy learned first aid from his father. He used a tourniquet to stop bleeding, treated rattlesnake bite by sucking out the poison, and sewed up cuts with cactus spines. The cause of a sickness, however, was not obvious.

The Comanche did not know that there are different diseases, each with a different cause and cure. If, for example, a patient burned with fever and shook with chills, it could mean only one thing: evil spirits were at work. This was a job for the medicine man. Using secret songs and charms, he tried to exorcise them, drive them out of the patient's body. Some patients improved, apparently because their faith in the "cure" helped their bodies resist the disease. Others got better because the disease went away by itself. Still others died.

Quanah grew wise in the ways of The People. He was said to be a handsome brave, a fine horseman, and a successful hunter by the age of fifteen. He had made medicine. Still, he had not killed a person or taken a scalp. Until he did so, he was of little account among the Nokoni. No one would ask his advice, and, although the girls might gaze at him from a distance, he was still not a fit husband.

Like all Comanche boys, Quanah yearned for the warpath. A brave with many scalps and many scars was to Quanah what an astronaut is to a twentieth-century youngster. He was a role model, to be admired and imitated. True, few braves reached old age. Quanah knew this, but it made no difference. He had been raised on The People's favorite proverb: "The brave die young." He expected to die in battle at an early age. That was good. Dying in battle meant dying honorably. Dying young meant dying while the body was strong and in its prime. A brave could ask no greater favor of the Great Spirit.

Old age held no appeal for Comanche boys. They saw nothing noble in growing old, and they dreaded it, for good reason. Life was a constant struggle for nomadic hunters. A man of forty was considered old; at fifty he was positively ancient. Women of twenty-five looked twice their age.

The older you were, the more difficult and painful life became. The elderly had to cope with failing health—toothaches, backaches, arthritis, blurred vision, stomach troubles, scars that hurt in cold weather. The hunter who could no longer hunt became a burden to his family. The warrior who could no longer take the warpath was no longer a whole man. His wives might leave him for younger men. Ambitious braves laughed, sure they could do better, when he boasted of his exploits. As an old person's health declined, he was "thrown away," abandoned by everyone. This was not due to lack of loyalty or kindness, but to fear. No one wanted to be invaded by the spirits that left a dying person's body. Sensing that the end was near, many old people wandered off to speak to the spirits one last time and to die alone.

Youths grew impatient for their first raid. Forming "gangs," they set out to find adventure and take scalps. They went with the blessings of their families. "At twelve or thirteen," Colonel Dodge wrote, "these yearlings can no longer be repressed; and banded together, the youths of from twelve to sixteen years roam over the country; and some of the most cold-blooded atrocities, daring attacks, and desperate combats, have been made by these children in pursuit of fame. From each of these excursions return, with crest erect and backbone stiffened, one or more youngsters, whose airs and style proclaim that each . . . is [a] candidate for the distinction of warrior."[20] If the council agreed, they joined the next war party.

Quanah would have enough adventures and war honors to satisfy the most hot-blooded of braves.

Interesting Times

"If I built a high wall between the red men and the white, the whites would scheme day and night to find a way around it."

—Sam Houston

THERE is an old Chinese curse that says: "May you live in interesting times." The ancients preferred dull times, times of peace and quiet, when people had only to be concerned with the ordinary things of life. Interesting times, however, were too strange, too exciting, too dangerous. They were the worst of times—times of war and famine and natural calamity. These were the times one wished upon enemies.

Quanah, most likely, never heard the curse. Had he done so, he would surely have understood its meaning. For he was a child of turmoil, born into one of the most interesting times in Comanche history. It all began at Fort Parker on that beautiful May day in 1836. The raid, and little Cynthia Ann's kidnapping, was a dividing line between old and new. On one side was the time when The People ruled the *Comanchería*. On the other side was the steady westward advance of the *tahbay-boh*, the palefaces. The resulting explosion would shake the Southwest for two generations.

Sam Houston, first president of the Texas Republic, had grown up among Indians in Tennessee. He liked them and understood them in a way few whites ever could. He had hoped to avoid trouble by trading with The People and avoiding their hunting grounds. Even such fierce warriors, he reasoned, would not fight if they could get the things they wanted peacefully.

Events at Fort Parker, however, prevented him from testing his idea. After the raid, the Texas frontier became a battleground. Comanche and Kiowa war parties swept down from the High Plains, striking the scattered settlements almost at will. It was a reign of terror. Raids, killings, and kidnappings became a regular part of frontier life. Rescuers, seeing smoke rising in the distance, arrived to find smoldering farmhouses and tortured, mutilated bodies. A frontier poem spoke of lost family and friends. One verse is about a bright youngster, full of hope and promise, whose life is suddenly cut short:

> He was young, and brave, and fair
> But the Indians raised his hair.[1]

Rachael Plummer's book also made a strong impression. Her description of the captives' sufferings inflamed Texans, fueling their desire to retaliate. Actually, it was more than a desire; it was a passion for revenge.

Houston's successor, Mirabeau B. Lamar, shared that passion. Only, for him, vengeance was not enough. Texas, he insisted, rightfully belonged to civilized people, not to "heathens" and "savages." The time had come for a final solution to the Indian problem. Lamar demanded "an exterminating war upon their warriors, which will admit of no compromise and have no termination except in their total extinction or total expulsion."[2] He meant every word. Slowly but surely, the tribes of eastern Texas—Wacos, Anadarkos, Ionis, Caddoes—were pushed across the border into the Indian Territory. Not that they were warlike; they seldom fought. But they were Indians, and that was enough for Lamar. The Comanche and Kiowa were another matter.

Early in 1840, three Penateka Comanche rode into San

Antonio to ask for a peace treaty. Townspeople had lived with war for four years; every day they passed the bullet-scarred ruins of the Alamo. Yes, said a government official, Texans, too, wanted peace. Yet no peace was possible until all white captives were returned to their families. The chiefs replied that they had already agreed among themselves to do that very thing. They left, promising to return in a few weeks to put their marks on a treaty.

On March 19, sixty-five Penatekas and one white prisoner, a girl, arrived. Dismounting, twelve chiefs filed into a courthouse known as the Council House. There they met a government delegation and a group of army officers. Fearing trouble, the officers had concealed troops near the building. Meantime, San Antonians gathered in the streets to gawk at the chiefs' families. They *were* a sight to see, those painted squaws and naked boys with miniature bows and arrows. Whites tossed coins in the air for the boys to shoot at. They never missed. The Comanches, for their part, had never seen so many *tahbay-boh* at once.

Their prisoner was Matilda Lockhart, sixteen, captured eighteen months earlier with four other children. Released as promised, she was taken to the home of Mary Maverick, wife of the town's leading merchant. Mrs. Maverick and her friends were horrified. The moment they saw Matilda, she burst into tears and said she was "utterly degraded, and could not hold up her head again." Not only had she been raped, her body was terribly disfigured. Mrs. Maverick recalled:

> She was in a frightful condition, poor girl, when at last she returned to civilization. Her head, arms, and face were full of bruises, and sores, and her nose actually burnt off to the bone—all the fleshy end gone, and a great scab formed on the end of the bone. Both nostrils were wide open and denuded of flesh. She told a piteous tale of how dreadfully the Indians had beaten her, and how they would wake her from sleep by sticking a chunk of fire on her flesh, especially to her nose, and how they would shout and laugh like fiends

when she cried. Her body had many scars from fire, many of which she showed us. Ah, it was sickening to behold, and made one's blood boil for vengeance.[3]

A few days earlier, Matilda, who had learned the Comanche tongue, overheard the chiefs discussing their plans for the meeting. Other prisoners, they said, were being held in other camps. Knowing how desperate Texans were for the return of their kinfolks, they meant to use them to their advantage. Rather than return them all at once, they would bargain for each one separately to get a higher ransom. Matilda's information was immediately sent to the Council House.

There the Texans seethed as Muk-war-rah, a famous medicine man, listed the chiefs' demands. To buy peace, he said, the Texans must give them ammunition, blankets, and other items. Comancheros had sold them guns, but there was always a shortage of bullets.

"Where are the prisoners you promised to bring into this talk?" asked a government agent, struggling to control his anger.

"We have brought in the only one we had," replied Muk-war-rah, arrogantly. "How do you like the answer?"[4]

They did not like it a bit. Soldiers filed into the room and took up positions along the walls. Then one of the government agents stood up. He told the chiefs they were under arrest. They would be jailed and held as hostages until every prisoner was safely returned. The interpreter refused to translate this, fearing he would be killed the moment he spoke. An officer insisted, and the interpreter edged closer to the door. Scarcely had the words left his mouth when he ran out of the room and down the street.

The chiefs, hearing their fate, shouted their war cries, drew their weapons, and sprang forward. It was the last thing they ever did. "Fire!" an officer cried. The room echoed with gunshots and filled with gray smoke. When the smoke cleared, all twelve chiefs and two whites lay dead. By then, however, blood was also flowing in the streets. Upon hearing the shots, the Comanche women and children turned on the white bystanders. A boy shot a toy arrow into the heart of a visiting judge, killing him instantly. Others were stabbed with knives or had their heads split open with hatchets. Soldiers, until then concealed behind buildings, opened fire on the Indians.

Those still on their feet tried to escape, soldiers and townspeople in hot pursuit. When the shooting began, Mary Maverick ran into her backyard after her two children, who were playing there. As she stepped outside, three braves dashed through the rear gate. "Here are Indians," she screamed, fearing the worst. Just then Mary's cook, a black slave named Jinny Anderson, stepped up with a rock in each hand. "If you don't go away from here I'll mash your head with this rock," Jinny cried. Few Comanches had ever seen a black person. And those who did, thought they were evil spirits. The braves ran away.[5]

The day ended with thirty-five Comanche killed, eight wounded, and the rest captured; seven Texans had died and eight were hurt. The town doctor would not let the Comanche dead rest in peace. He came up to Mary's window and, with a deep bow, put two bloody heads on the sill. He had selected these heads, a brave's and a squaw's, for scientific study, he said, looking very pleased with himself. He had also put aside two bodies, a male and a female, to be boiled down for their skeletons.[6]

The Texans sent a squaw back to the Plains with an ultimatum. She was to tell The People that unless all prisoners were released their captured relatives would be executed. News of the "Council House Fight" struck the Comanche camps like a bolt of lightning. Nothing like it had ever happened before. The loss of life was a catastrophe greater than any suffered in a whole year's raiding into Mexico. Worse, the Texans had broken a sacred, solemn truce. Such treachery was beyond belief. It violated everything Indians cherished—hospitality, honor, honesty. No one could remember a Plains tribe turning upon guests.

The People's grief was directed against their helpless captives. A boy named Booker Webster later told what happened.

Luckily for Booker, he had just been adopted by a Comanche family. His fellow captives had not. All of them, about twenty in number, were tortured to death by squaws; Matilda Lockhart's six-year-old sister was among the victims.[7] The Texas authorities, however, could not bring themselves to kill prisoners in cold blood. Eventually, they gave them to San Antonio families as servants. All escaped.

Meantime, Indian raids grew in size and fury. Their way lit by the Comanche Moon, war parties could now choose among enemies. Continuing to torment northern Mexico, they might just as easily strike deep into Texas, encouraged by Comancheros eager to buy stolen property. Over a thousand raiders rode as far as Linneville, a tiny port on the Gulf of Mexico. Fleeing to boats in the harbor, townspeople watched helplessly as warriors burned their homes and took away hundreds of horses loaded with loot.[8] Nevertheless, townspeople felt lucky to escape with their lives. "*Tejanos*"—Texans—could expect no mercy from The People.

Nor could the raiders expect mercy from the Texans. Fort Parker had lit a flame. The Council House Fight had whipped that flame into a tornado of hatred.

The Comanche way of war astonished the Texans. It was not their way. Texans felt that a battle should be a shooting match between armies that could be plainly seen and easily identified. That was how Europeans fought, and how they had won their independence from Mexico. The word "terrorism" had not yet been invented, but Texans would have understood its meaning. Their enemies made war by stealth, surprise, ambush, torture, kidnapping, and the murder of women and children. President Lamar, Texans agreed, was right. Indians were "savages," "brutes," "beasts," "monsters," "vermin," and "demons in human form." Mother Nature made them that way, since, a soldier noted, "the cruelty of the Indian is born in and bred with him, and clings to him through life."[9] And if Indians were scarcely human, it followed that the rules of "civilized warfare" did not apply to them. It must be a struggle to the death.

✕   ✕   ✕

Texans were already preparing for that struggle. Six months after Fort Parker, their congress passed a law creating units of "Mounted Riflemen, now and hereafter [to be] in the ranging service on the frontier."[10] Those in the ranging service were called "rangers"—Texas Rangers. Rangers are an old and honored tradition in North America. During the French and Indian War (1756–1763), the British sent Rogers's Rangers on surprise attacks behind enemy lines in New York and Canada. In the American Revolution (1775–1783), Francis Marion, the famed "Swamp Fox," led hit-and-run raids on the British from his base in the South Carolina swamps. That tradition is carried on by today's Army Rangers and Navy SEALs (Sea-Air-Land forces).

The Texas Rangers "ranged"; that is, covered thousands of square miles of frontier on horseback. Unlike a regular army occupying a given area, they were constantly on the move, constantly searching for trouble. They had a threefold mission: patrolling to give early warning of a raid, pursuing raiders after they struck, and preventing raids by striking would-be raiders first.

The mission required a special breed of men. A fellow in his late teens or early twenties, the typical ranger was an adventurer, without family or property, who loved action and hated Indians. A do-it-yourself fighter, he provided his own horse, weapons, and clothing; uniforms were not issued. His usual outfit, one recalled, was "buckskin moccasins and overalls, a roundabout and red shirt, a cap manufactured by his own hands from the skin of a coon or a wildcat, three revolvers and a bowie knife in his belt, and a short rifle on his arm."[11] Courage was taken for granted in that brotherhood of fighting men. Cowards did not

A Texas Ranger as he appeared in a drawing done about the year 1840. A mounted gunman who "ranged" far and wide, the Ranger gave early warning of Indian raids to settlers and carried the fight to the enemy in swift hit-and-run raids.

Colonel John Coffee Hays of the Texas Rangers. At the Battle of the Pedernales, Hays and his men introduced the Comanche to Samuel Colt's six-shooter.

become Texas Rangers, or survive very long in the service.

Not one to miss a good time when off duty, the ranger was all business while in action. Unlike the Indian brave, who fought for personal glory, he was a team player. He had to be; since ranger companies were nearly always outnumbered, teamwork was their best hope of survival. Teamwork required obedience to commands, which in turn demanded firm leadership. Company captains were the backbone of the Texas Rangers. Natural leaders, they inspired others to instant, unquestioning obedience.

The greatest of them was John Coffee Hays. A captain at twenty-two, "Captain Jack," as everyone called him, did not look like a tough fighter. Thin and smooth-shaven, with delicate hands and a high-pitched voice, he was always calm and self-controlled, a tower of strength to his men. In battle, he was not a "go-there" commander, but a "follow-me" commander. He led from the front, never asking anybody to do anything he would not do himself—and do it first. Even braves, who knew about courage, admired him. "Me and Red Wing not afraid to go to hell together," said Chief Flacco of the Apache. "Captain Jack heap brave; not afraid to go to hell by himself." Other Indians, less complimentary, called him the "little white devil."[12]

It was by no means certain, in 1840, that the Texans would win. Firepower was the problem. A Texas Ranger carried a pistol and a long-barreled musket. Fired at close range, their round lead slugs could tear off an arm or punch a hole in a man's chest the size of an apple. But they were heavy weapons and difficult to reload; an expert could shoot twice a minute, and that only with both legs planted firmly on the ground, because the bullet had to be loaded through the muzzle. Used while racing across the Plains on horseback, such weapons were practically worthless. Having fired his single shot, a ranger was in big trouble.

The brave carried weapons designed for fast-paced action in the saddle. A mounted Comanche could cover three hundred yards in a minute. If the ranger turned to flee, the brave simply lanced him from behind. If the ranger stopped to reload, the brave, who could put eight arrows in flight at once, turned him into a human pincushion. Nor was there safety in numbers. A war party would encircle a group of rangers to draw their fire, and when their guns were empty charge as they were reloading. The ranger's only chance was to dismount and take cover behind a pile of rocks, rare things on the High Plains. Some desperate men shot their horses and hid behind their bodies. They might drive off their attackers, only to find that their troubles had only just begun. A man on foot was helpless on the Plains, where thirst and exhaustion quickly turned him into buzzard bait.

Samuel Colt rescued the Texas frontier. In 1836, he opened a factory to manufacture his invention in Paterson, New Jersey. The invention was the revolver, known as "the peacemaker" and "the gun that won the West." Lightweight and easy to use, the revolver was actually six pistols in one. A man armed with Colt's "six-shooter" or "six-gun" could fire six times before having to reload. Yet business was slow at first; Colt's most likely customer, the U.S. Army, saw no need for the weapon, and he faced bankruptcy. But somehow a few samples found their way to Captain Jack's headquarters in San Antonio. The rangers' problem was solved instantly. Orders were placed for more pistols, and a grateful Colt named his favorite model the "Texas."

The six-shooter was put to the test on June 8, 1844. Hays was leading a fourteen-man patrol when they were jumped near the Pedernales River northwest of San Antonio. Seventy-five Comanches burst from ambush, shouting war cries and filling the air with arrows. They had made good medicine and were sure of taking many scalps, as they had done so often in the past.

But how wrong they were! Instead of dashing for cover, as expected, Hays turned and charged head-on. Warriors were stunned as rangers met them face-to-face and knee to knee. Hays's men pushed ahead, streaks of flame leaping from their fists. Comanches tumbled to the ground with torn chests and shattered skulls. Their medicine broken, their comrades wheeled and fled for their lives. Left behind were thirty Comanche bodies, a frightful loss for any band. Two rangers died. Never again did their chief want to fight these demons, who had "a shot for every finger of the hand." Colt honored the rangers by engraving scenes from the Battle of the Pedernales on the barrels of a special edition of his six-shooter. It was also good publicity and, before long, the U.S. Army adopted the weapon.

Texas Rangers believed that the best defense is a good offense. Having mastered the six-shooter, they began to take the war to the enemy. They fought Comanche style, traveling lightly, moving fast, and striking sleeping camps at dawn. Captain "Rip" Ford described how they lived and fought:

> [The ranger] would put a layer of grass, or small brush, beneath his pallet, to avoid being chilled by the cold ground, and to prevent his blankets from becoming saturated in case of rain. His gun coat was placed over his saddle and rigging; his gun was by his side; his coat, boots and pistols were used as a pillow; his rations were fastened to his saddle; his head was to the north, and his feet to the fire, if he dared to have one. Generally he slept with most of his clothes on—ready to spring up and fight at a moment's notice. The least noise—of an unusual nature—would wake him, and in an instant he would be in fighting trim. In the warfare of those days it was victory or death. . . . The one idea rules—make a rapid, noiseless march—strike the foe while he was not on the alert—punish him—crush him! With many there was a vengeful spirit to urge them on. Mothers, sisters, fathers, brothers, had been inhumanely butchered and scalped. Loved relatives had been captured, enslaved and outraged, and the memory of the cruel past rose up before the mind's eye, and goaded them into action. They fearlessly plunged into the thickest of the fight, and struck for vengeance.[13]

Women were killed during these swift assaults. The reason, in part, is that it was often impossible to tell a squaw from a brave in the confusion of a dawn attack. If you did see a woman, chances were she was shooting at you. And she could shoot straight!

There was another reason for killing Comanche women and, yes, children. War is always brutalizing. Yet nothing is so brutalizing as fighting an enemy who is very different from yourself and who fights by different rules. Indians ignored the rules of "civilized" warfare; that is, they did not follow the rules as laid down by whites. As a result, rangers saw nothing wrong in paying them back in kind. They adopted some of the enemy's most horrible practices, particularly scalping. Some regretted it years later, when the Comanche threat had passed and they could quietly reflect on what they had done. But at the time, they were ruthless, even "savage." Ranger Ed Carnal recalled: "We rangers, as well as Indians, fought under the black flag. We asked no quarter and gave none. When we fell into their hands they scalped us and frightfully mutilated our bodies, frequently cutting and hacking us to pieces. We didn't do as bad as that but scalped them just the same. Indian scalps in ranger camps were as common as pony tracks."[14]

✕ ✕ ✕

Quanah was a baby when Texas joined the Union on December 29, 1845. The following spring, a dispute over the southern border of Texas exploded into war between the United States and Mexico. Defeated by 1847, Mexico gave up its claim to all lands north of the Rio Grande, or about half its national territory, a loss that still stirs anger.

Victory was a bonanza for the United States. In return for $15 million in gold, it gained 1.2 million square miles of land, including Texas. The nation's area grew by at least a third, its east-west boundaries extending from the Atlantic to the Pacific Ocean. The new territories included all of the future states of California, Nevada, and Utah, nearly all of Arizona and New Mexico, plus part of Colorado and Wyoming. Life for the Plains Indians would never be the same.

The Comanche had befriended the Americans during the war. Government agents gave them gifts, encouraging them to continue raiding into Mexico. Though Americans and Texans spoke English, the Comanche saw a big difference between them. Americans seemed generous and friendly; the *Tejanos* were proven enemies who killed chiefs at council meetings. They continued to help the one while fighting the other.

Peace with Mexico affected the Plains tribes in unexpected ways. Almost immediately, rich farmlands became available in Oregon and gold was discovered in California. Each year, for the next ten years, thousands of settlers passed along two well-known highways. The Oregon Trail led across the northern Plains to Wyoming, through South Pass in the Rockies, and onward to the Oregon country. Forty-niners sought their El Dorado, their kingdom of gold, by heading south. The El Dorado Trail crossed the Rio Grande at El Paso, Texas, winding westward across Mexico to California.

Trail life could be a real adventure. Travelers were amazed at the sea of grass and the buffalo herds stretching to the horizon and beyond. More often than not, however, the journey was a dangerous, exhausting ordeal that could last a year before the travelers saw the Promised Lands—*if* they lived to see them.

Both trails crossed the buffalo range. Emigrants usually traveled together for safety, hundreds of people in each wagon train. Their coming was like a plague spreading across the face of the earth. Emigrants knew little, and cared less, about the ecology of the Great Plains. Wherever they halted, the land died. Left behind were heaps of stinking garbage, rusty cans, dead oxen, polluted water holes, and river bottoms stripped of their timber.

The rumble of heavy "prairie schooners" scared the game; the emigrants' bullets killed them in droves. Animals learned to avoid the trails, grazing farther to the north or south. "All experience proves that the game rapidly disappears before the firearms of the white," noted Thomas A. Harvey, a government agent. "He kills for the sake of killing."[15] The buffalo-hunting tribes felt the impact. Herds failed to visit their usual grazing grounds, forcing the hunters to travel farther and search longer for food, then only to find the ground littered with rotting carcasses.

The emigrants also brought their germs. Disease and conquest had always marched together in the New World. Epidemics of smallpox did more to destroy the Aztecs of Mexico and the Incas of Peru than all the conquistadores' guns and swords. Whites had been exposed to the great killer diseases—smallpox, cholera, measles, mumps, scarlet fever, whooping cough—since ancient times. Many still died, of course, but the majority survived after running a high fever, due to immunities built up over so many centuries. But these diseases were unknown to Native Americans before 1492. So, lacking any natural immunity, they were devastated when whites carried the germs inland. In this way, every trail across the Great Plains became a highway for spreading disease.

Young Quanah was lucky: he and his family survived. We do not know how they did it, or how many of the Nokoni Comanche died. Quanah was probably too young to remember those times; or if he did, he never spoke of them for the record.

Thousands of families perished in the decade following the Mexican War. In the northern Plains, smallpox spared a mere hundred Mandans out of sixteen hundred, and may well have killed half the Blackfeet. The Minnetaree, Assiniboin, Pawnee, Crow, and Arikara were hit equally hard.[16] In the southern Plains, fully half the Comanche died of cholera brought by Forty-niners. Kiowa losses were at least as great.[17] Compared to disease, the tribes' war losses were minor. Bacteria, not bullets, were the chief killers of Native Americans.

No "medicine" could ward off the diseases or cure them once they took hold. When disease struck a village, panic spread like wildfire. Unable to help themselves, or even understand what was happening to them, people lost control. Colonel Dodge saw the results with his own eyes:

To describe the superstitious terror . . . is beyond the power of words. . . . A wail of utter despair ascends to heaven. Camps and lodges are abandoned, the dead and dying left unburied and uncared for, and those not afflicted, breaking up into families, fly in every direction from the scene of suffering. . . . An unfortunate seized with the disease en route is forced to leave the party, to live or die solitary and alone in the wilderness. Husbands abandon their wives, children their aged parents, mothers their nursing infants, and this terrible race for life continues until the disease has worn itself out, either from want of contact or lack of victims. The places at which these terrible visitations have overtaken the Indians are forever regarded with superstitious terror, and no persuasion or bribe could induce an Indian, knowingly, to visit them.[18]

Meantime, Quanah's people changed their opinion of the Americans. The peace treaty with Mexico had pledged the United States to stop Indian raids south of the Rio Grande. By the late 1840s, army forts were being built at key points along the Great Comanche War Trail and at the Rio Grande crossings. A second group of forts was built farther to the east, to guard the Texas settlements. Now soldiers visited Indian encampments, not with smiling faces and tempting gifts, but to tell them how to live.

To the Comanche and Kiowa, it was ridiculous to ask them to give up their old ways. They had been raiding Mexico for over a century. Raiding was their way of life, their birthright. And not even the Great White Father in Washington, the president of the United States, could keep them from taking vengeance on the hated *Tejanos*. By protecting Mexicans and Texans, the Americans had shown they were enemies.

The American military did not seem dangerous. True, they had whipped the Mexicans, but the Comanche had always done that. Although soldiers outnumbered the Texas Rangers, they lacked their Indian-fighting skills. The army had fought forest Indians back east, but it had no experience with "horse Indians."

It didn't even have cavalry, forces specially trained to fight on horseback. Cavalry were expensive, and Congress did not want to spend the money. The yearly cost of a cavalry regiment was $1.5 million, five times that of an infantry regiment.

Foot soldiers held the forts, but they were useless on the Plains. Braves called them "walk-a-heaps" and pitied their sore feet. The dragoons, mounted infantrymen armed with swords and rifles, were no better. Dragoons did not fight in the saddle, but rode to the scene of action and dismounted to meet the enemy on foot. They were no threat to the Comanche, who could ride circles around them in their sleep. The only danger, said a Texas Ranger, was that braves might laugh themselves to death at the sight of dragoons.

Jefferson Davis was not amused. As president of the Confederacy during the Civil War, he was branded a traitor to the United States. But all that lay in the future. In 1853, he was a respected politician and secretary of war. Realizing that it took mounted men to beat mounted men, he persuaded Congress to create two cavalry regiments. The Second Cavalry was known as "Jeff Davis's Own," because he personally selected its officers. He chose carefully and well—*very* well. Many of his appointees would wear general's stars during the Civil War. The majority fought for the Confederacy, including the regiment's colonel, Albert Sidney Johnston, and its lieutenant colonel, Robert E. Lee. There was also Major Earl van Dorn, Captain Edmund Kirby-Smith, and Lieutenant John Bell Hood. Major George H. Thomas served the Union, becoming famous as the "Rock of Chickamauga."

The Second Cavalry went to Texas. Its officers made mistakes at first, as was to be expected. But they learned from these mistakes, and from the Texas Rangers. Before long, they had the Comanche on the run.

Cavalry units and ranger units operated together. Instead of pursuing separate war parties, they went to the source of the trouble: the enemy camps. Not that these camps were easy to get

The Trooper, a drawing by Frederic Remington for the magazine *Cavalry Journal*. The cavalry-man was armed with a six-shooter and a carbine, a light-weight rifle with a short barrel. He did not carry a sword into battle, because that would have been useless at close range against the Indian's fourteen-foot buffalo lance.

at. Concealed along sheltered streams or located far out on the High Plains, finding them was work for the scouts, Indians hired to fight other Indians. These men did not consider themselves traitors to their own kind; there was no such thing as an "Indian nation," only separate tribes and bands. The People had made enemies during their march of conquest. Some enemies, like the Tonkawa, bore grudges and burned for revenge. Nicknamed "Tonks," they were a small tribe that had nearly been exterminated by the lords of the *Comanchería*.

Dozens of cavalry and ranger patrols left the forts each month. Some skirted the settlements, providing an early-warning system. Others probed the eastern edges of the *Comanchería*. Moving cautiously, they sought to catch the enemy off guard, preferably at dawn. When they did, they hit fast, hit hard, and kept on hitting. In a series of punishing attacks, encampments were overrun by shouting horsemen with blazing six-guns. Little, if any, effort was made to show mercy. Certain raids, in fact, came close to being massacres. In the words of General Persifor F. Smith: "It is not deemed advisable to take prisoners."[19] In effect, the American fighting man had a license to kill Indians.

By 1857, on the eve of the Civil War, the Comanche were feeling the strain. White diseases had taken a frightful toll. White soldiers were striking without letup. Only the Quahadi band, safe amid the vastness of the Staked Plain, was as aggressive as ever. Not being suicidal, their brothers to the east went on the defensive. Raiding into Mexico all but ceased. War parties avoided Texas settlements like the plague, attacking only isolated ranches. But even this was dangerous; cowboys usually carried two six-shooters, and knew how to use them.

Early in May 1858, when Quanah was thirteen, the Nokoni were hunting in the Indian Territory. They were led by Iron Jacket, a famous chief who wore a piece of armor taken from the remains of a long-dead conquistador discovered on the Plains. Since the armor was strong medicine, Iron Jacket took charge of the main camp spread along the north bank of the Canadian River. Peta Nocona was camped with his people a few miles upstream, in the Antelope Hills.

The Nokoni had no idea that Captain John S. Ford was coming with 215 Texas Rangers and Tonkawa scouts. Nicknamed "Old Rip" because he signed his casualty reports with the letters RIP ("Rest in Peace"), Ford was one of the rangers' most aggressive captains. He aimed to demolish the Nokoni.

The rangers splashed across the shallow Canadian at dawn on May 12. Undetected, they were moving into attack position when their overeager scouts destroyed a small encampment two miles below Iron Jacket's. Two braves escaped on horseback and gave the alarm.

It was like throwing a stone into a beehive. Hundreds of angry warriors swarmed from their tipis, smearing on black paint as squaws caught and saddled their mounts. As the rangers approached, they put on a dazzling display of horsemanship. Some braves rode backward, waving weapons and making obscene gestures with their fingers. Others dropped over the sides of their mounts, then stood on their backs like circus riders. The outnumbered Texans halted to watch the show and get ready for action. But these were veterans, and it took a lot to impress them. Calmly, bearded men in red flannel shirts spat streams of chewing tobacco and slid six-shooters from holsters.

Iron Jacket rode toward the waiting rangers. Sure of his medicine, he challenged Old Rip to personal combat. The captain had other plans. He raised his right arm and brought it down sharply. Shots rang out. Iron Jacket fell dead. The Texans charged. Seeing their chief's medicine broken, the Nokoni lost heart. Fighting only to cover their families' escape, they abandoned the camp. A running battle followed, in which parties of rangers chased groups of braves over the countryside. Ford's orders were to press the assault, preventing the scattered braves from joining forces. By the afternoon, seventy-six warriors and two rangers lay dead. Old Rip had won a stunning victory.

He would have won a total victory had it not been for Peta Nocona. Hearing distant gunfire, he gathered his braves and sped toward the sound. Though still a boy, Quanah probably rode with them; faced with such danger, every able-bodied male was expected to defend the camp. Youngsters, indeed, longed for a chance to prove themselves. Anyone left behind would have felt, and have been *made* to feel, cowardly.

The rangers had not known about this reserve force. Its sudden appearance convinced Ford to withdraw while he was still ahead. Peta Nocona was the hero of the day. With Iron Jacket gone, he became the Nokonis' supreme war chief and the most feared warrior on the High Plains. For the next two and a half years, he led war parties against the Texans; indeed, one passed close to the site of old Fort Parker. Quanah was learning from a master.

Peta Nocona's reputation also meant trouble. His growing fame made every Indian fighter want a crack at him. Their chance came toward the end of 1860. December 18 was an ominous day for both Nokonis and Americans. The United States was falling apart. That very morning, a convention was meeting in Columbia, South Carolina, to discuss leaving the Union. Three days later, South Carolina seceded, soon to be joined by other Southern states. Eleven states in all, including Texas, formed a new nation called the Confederate States of America. The Civil War was about to begin.

A combined force of cavalry and rangers found the Nokoni camp on the Pease River, a branch of the Red River, in the Texas Panhandle. Few braves were present, most having joined the chief and his sons to follow a buffalo herd. The squaws had already broken camp and were moving out when a norther swept through the area. The cold wind howled, filling the air with swirling sand. Unable to see or hear the oncoming enemy, they were taken completely by surprise.

This was a small raid, but one incident was to make it

famous. Rangers led by Captain Lawrence Sullivan ("Sul") Ross passed through some squaws and shot the braves as they came up on them. Cavalrymen led by a sergeant fell in behind the rangers, killing all the squaws, almost in a pile. Ross, meantime, was chasing two riders up ahead. One had a "boy" behind him on the saddle, the other followed by a few yards on a gray horse. Nearing the second horse, Ross was about to pull the trigger when the rider, a woman, held up a baby and came to a halt. Ross ordered an aide, Lieutenant Tom Kelliheir, to look after them; he knew the cavalry was killing squaws and wanted to spare the mother and baby.

Ross overtook the other horse and opened fire, bringing down the "boy" with his first bullet. But as the victim fell, he saw it was a Mexican girl of about fifteen. As she fell, she pulled the man off. He rolled on the ground, regained his feet, and sent a flock of arrows whizzing past the ranger's head. A load of buckshot fired by a scout finished him off. The whole incident lasted less than three minutes from start to finish.

The fight over, the victors headed back to their campsite in a clump of cottonwoods along the stream. They rode in a straight line, trampling the dead squaws under their horses' hooves. Not everyone was pleased with the day's work. "I was in the Pease River fight," recalled ranger H. B. Rogers, "but I am not very proud of it. That was not a battle at all, but just a killing of squaws. One or two bucks [braves] and sixteen squaws were killed."[20]

Ross joined the lieutenant and his prisoners. Kelliheir was swearing at himself for having ridden his best horse so hard after an "old squaw." She was very dirty, her hands and clothes darkened by smoke and buffalo grease. But as soon as he saw her face, Old Rip knew she was special. "Why, Tom," he said, "this is a white woman, Indians do not have blue eyes."[21]

Could this be Cynthia Ann Parker? Ross thought so. Upon returning to his post, he sent for Colonel Isaac Parker, her father's older brother and a Texas state senator. He came at once, bringing an interpreter.

Opposite page: Cynthia Ann Parker, called Naduah, and her daughter, Topsannah, or Prairie Flower, were photographed soon after their capture by Texas Rangers. As with all Comanche women, Cynthia's hair was worn long; but after capture, she cut it short as a sign of mourning.

Ross and Kelliheir took them to the captive's tent. Colonel Parker looked at her carefully, but could not be sure of her identity. The last time he saw Cynthia Ann, she was a rosy-cheeked girl of nine. Here was a dark-skinned woman with a baby in her arms. She spoke no English. All she did was cry and make motions as if she wanted to return to the Plains.

"Colonel," said Kelliheir, "it appears to me that the last thing she would remember of her home life would be the name that her family called her."

"I do know well that my brother and his wife called her Cynthia Ann," the colonel replied.

Cynthia Ann! The words were an echo of the past, stirring deep memories. She rose and patted her breast, saying: "Me Cincee Ann."

The interpreter spoke with her for several minutes. Satisfied at last, he told the others: "She says that she much regrets it, but it is a fact that she had a paleface pa and a paleface ma, and they had a name for her, and that name was Cincee Ann. She says that now, though, she has a redman pa and a redman ma." Questioned further, she described Fort Parker and recalled being captured twenty-five years earlier.[22]

Colonel Parker took her to his home near Fort Worth. During a visit to town, he had a photograph taken of her while nursing the infant Prairie Flower. The photograph shows a sad-looking woman with her hair cut short, as if in mourning. She had plenty to be sad about. Never again would she see her husband and sons.

Peta Nocona returned to his camp to find the ground strewn with bodies. The chief was heartbroken and, Quanah recalled, "shed many tears" over the loss of Naduah and the death of the Mexican girl, who turned out to be his second wife. He never married again.[23] Three years later, wounded and dying, he told Quanah that his mother was a white woman. Until then, both sons had known only that she was Naduah, a woman of The People. Quanah's brother, Pecos, died shortly after his father.

Naduah had lost everything—twice. First, as Cynthia Ann Parker, she had been taken from the world into which she had been born. Adjusting to another world, she was snatched from that as well. But she could not return to the white world. Though the Parkers made every effort to be kind, they could not give her what she really wanted: freedom to live the life she had known for a quarter of a century. They could not imagine that the worst tragedy in her life was not being kidnapped and raised as a Comanche, but being taken from her Comanche family. That she wanted to go back only proved she was unfit to make her own decisions. Incredibly lonely, considering herself a prisoner, she would sit at a window for hours, sobbing, Prairie Flower in her arms. Several times she stole a horse and tried to escape, only to be caught.

One day a Confederate agent named Coho Smith visited Colonel Parker's house. With the Civil War raging, the Confederacy wanted Comanchero aid in smuggling supplies across New Mexico, which had sided with the Union. During lunch, Smith tried to speak to Cynthia Ann in Spanish. She became frantic. Leaping from her seat, she swept the dishes off the table and cried: *"Mi corazón está llorando todo el tiempo por mis dos hijos!"*—"My heart always weeps for my two sons!"[24] She begged Smith to help her escape, promising that The People—her people—would give anything for her return.

It was not to be. In December 1863, little Prairie Flower died of a fever. The grieving mother lost interest in life. She died the following October of a combination of self-starvation and influenza. Some said she died of a broken heart.

✹ ✹ ✹

The Civil War was a disaster for settlers throughout the West. When it began in April 1861, the frontier army all but melted away. The best units were ordered east, to the battlefields in Virginia and the Mississippi Valley. Before long, the tribes were running riot across the Plains. From north to south, from the Dakota Territory to the Rio Grande, whites went in fear of their lives. In Minnesota, the Santee Sioux under Chief Little Crow carried out the greatest Indian massacre in American history, killing nearly a thousand settlers before being defeated by a volunteer force. The Ute took the warpath in Idaho, as did the Navajo in New Mexico and the Apache in Arizona. In Utah, Utes and Shoshones hit wagon trains and cut telegraph lines. The Cheyenne and Arapaho attacked mining camps in Colorado, isolating Denver for days at a time.

The Lone Star State suffered terribly. There were simply not enough able-bodied men to defend so large a frontier area. Most Texas Rangers had joined the Confederate army immediately after secession, while the Second Cavalry split between Union and Confederate sympathizers. Many Union loyalists were able to leave the state, but others became prisoners of war. All the frontier forts were abandoned. Except for a handful of local volunteers, greenhorns at Indian fighting, the frontier was unprotected.

The Comanche and Kiowa took the offensive. War parties rampaged across western Texas, killing, looting, and burning. The fearless traveler—and there were very few of these—found only desolation. The frontier collapsed as the line of white settlement was pushed eastward up to two hundred miles.[25] You could ride for days without seeing a white person or an intact house. Thousands of families had packed up and fled to the larger towns. Not all left in time, however; scores of women and children were taken prisoner, their cries echoing across the Valley of Tears as never before. A federal official wrote of the Kiowa: "They boastfully say that stealing white women is a more lucrative business than stealing horses."[26]

The government in Washington was partly responsible for this terrorism. Its army purchasing agents in New Mexico were offering top dollar for cattle, with no questions asked. Happy to oblige, the Comancheros urged their friends to seize *Tejano* herds. To counter the whites' superior firepower, they traded Colt six-shooters and ten-shot Winchester repeating rifles for stolen cattle. And if braves had nothing to trade, or were short of ammunition, Comancheros lent them what they needed to go on a raid.

Such "generosity" paid off. At least three hundred thousand head of cattle stolen in Texas were sold in New Mexico during the Civil War. Yet not all rustlers belonged to war parties. Gangs of white outlaws roamed the Plains at will, disguised as Indians. An official report noted that one gang was led by a "blue-eyed, red-headed Indian!" Elsewhere, two "braves" shot during a raid were found, on close examination, to be whites in breechclouts and moccasins. Outlaws also acted as go-betweens in returning kidnapped whites, for ransom, to their families. Some, indeed, were accused of leading Comanches on kidnapping raids.[27]

With the defeat of the Confederacy in 1865, the federal government wanted to end frontier violence. Three years earlier, Congress had passed the Homestead Act, which President Lincoln signed "so that every poor man may have a home," and laws for building a transcontinental railroad. A new flood of emigrants was expected, and with them still more trouble with the Plains tribes.

A congressional committee was appointed to study the causes of Indian warfare and suggest remedies. It offered only two choices. The first choice, using force, was expensive. Conquering horse Indians would take at least ten thousand soldiers, create a war lasting three years, and cost over thirty million dollars.[28] The second choice, making a peace treaty, was cheaper and safer. The White House agreed. In the fall of 1867, a seven-member peace commission was sent to meet with the tribes. Four commission members were civilians and three military men, including General William Tecumseh Sherman, general in chief of the United States Army.

In October 1867, the commission arrived at Medicine Lodge Creek in southern Kansas. Thousands of Comanches, Kiowas,

Kiowa-Apaches, Cheyennes, and Arapahoes were waiting to meet them.[29]

Quanah watched from a nearby ridge. It was a breathtaking scene, one he would carry with him for the rest of his days. Tipis were spread out along the creek as far as the eye could see, with herds of horses grazing on the Plains beyond. It seemed as if all the people and all the horses on earth had gathered at this spot.

The commissioners were escorted by five hundred soldiers dressed exactly alike, in blue uniforms with shiny brass buttons and black boots, and a column of wagons two miles long. The tribesmen gave them a show the likes of which few whites had seen and lived to tell about. Quanah watched as thousands of armed warriors rode forward in a V-formation. Attack formation!

Shouting and waving feather banners, they formed two lines and began circling from right and left. Faster and faster they rode, a blur of whirling figures. Closer and closer they came. The *tahbay-boh* dropped to one knee, aimed their rifles, and waited for orders. The warriors halted only yards away from the soldiers. Experienced officers ordered their men to fall in. They could see that the braves were wearing bright war paint, but there was no trace of black—the death color. They did not mean to fight. It was only a greeting, and a test of the whites' good faith. Had any soldier lost his nerve and fired, there would have been a battle.

Reporters described their visits to the Indian camps in articles for readers back east. "Five thousand Indians," one wrote, "have assembled . . . in their glory of paint, rags, deerskin leggings, vermin-covered blankets, and dirty bodies, never washed except by the rains of heaven."[30] There *was* plenty of dirt. Garbage of every description—rotting bits of buffalo meat, cracked bones, lengths of intestine—lay about, smelling to high heaven.

They also noted that everything was orderly, if a bit noisy.

General William Tecumseh Sherman was one of the Union's best officers during the Civil War. After the war, he took command of the troops sent West to crush Indian resistance.

Industrious squaws were busy mending clothes, cooking, gathering wood, and tanning buffalo hides. Some held squirming children as they picked lice from their hair. Groups of warriors, many with deep smallpox scars on their faces, stood about talking. Everyone looked up when a boy accidentally fired a six-shooter while cleaning it. Seeing there was no danger, they went about their business as if nothing had happened. It was taken for granted that youngsters should occasionally hurt themselves while handling firearms. Wounds were simply part of growing up. Nothing to worry about.[31]

Quanah was fascinated by the strangers, being half white himself. When Comanches visited the army camp, he made sure to go along. Like them, he made himself at home, walking into tents unannounced. And, like them, he lined up at the huge iron kettles for that marvelous brew, coffee, army cooks were handing out in tin mugs. After emptying their mugs, the tribesmen ran their fingers around the bottom, collecting the leftover sugar on their fingertips.

Quanah, however, had another reason for going. Hoping to learn what had happened to his mother, he introduced himself to Philip McClusker, an interpreter married to a Comanche woman. McClusker told him of his mother's return to her white family and that she was no longer alive. To show his undying love, the brave took her family name. From then on, he would be known as Quanah Parker.[32]

Quanah Parker heard the speeches at the peace council. The commissioners said the Great Father, the president of the United States, loved his red children so much that he wanted to protect them from the *tahbay-boh*. The tribes would be given their own country, a reservation in the Indian Territory, far away from the settlements. No whites would trouble them there; the army would see to that. And no expense would be spared to give them houses, barns, blacksmith shops, hospitals, schools, and churches. To help them become farmers, they would receive seeds, cattle, sheep, and instruction in farming. Each year, for thirty years, twenty-five thousand dollars' worth of clothing and other useful things would be distributed. In return, they must stop fighting the whites, promise not to take any more white captives, and not interfere with the railroads and forts that would be built in their country. They would, however, be allowed to hunt on their old lands "so long as the buffalo may range thereon."

There was silence as the first speaker, Satanta of the Kiowa, rose to his feet. A tall man with black hair reaching down to his shoulders, Satanta was a famous warrior. He reminded the commissioners that the Kiowa were hunters and fighters, not farmers. Farming was for women, living in houses for weaklings who could not stand the wind on their faces. Onlookers, Quanah Parker among them, nodded their approval.

Par-roowah Sermehno, or Ten Bears, spoke next. An elderly man with wrinkled skin, he spoke eloquently for the Yamparika Comanche—so eloquently, in fact, that his speech was translated and printed in the newspapers.

> My heart is filled with joy when I see you here, as the brooks fill with water when the snows melt in the spring; and I feel glad as the ponies do when the fresh grass starts in the beginning of the year. . . . My people have never first drawn a bow or fired a gun against the whites. There had been trouble . . . between us, and my young men have danced the war dance. But it was not begun by us. . . . So it was in Texas. They made sorrow come to our camps, and we went out like the buffalo bulls when the cows are attacked. When we found them we killed them, and their scalps hang in our lodges. The Comanches are not weak and blind, like the pups of a dog when seven sleeps old. They are strong and far-sighted, like grown horses. We

The Kiowa chief Satanta took his own life after being sent to prison for massacring a group of army wagon drivers in Texas.

took their road and we went on it. The white women cried
and our women laughed.

But there are things which you have said to me which I
do not like. They are not sweet like sugar, but bitter like
gourds. You said that you wanted to put us on a reservation,
to build us houses and make us medicine lodges [hospitals].
I do not want them. I was born on the prairie, where the
wind blew free and there was nothing to break the light of
the sun. I was born where there were no enclosures and
where everything drew a free breath. I want to die there and
not within walls. I know every stream and every wood
between the Rio Grande and the Arkansas. I have hunted
and lived over that country. I lived like my fathers before me
and like them I lived happily. . . . So, why do you ask us to
leave the rivers, and the sun, and the wind, and live in houses? Do not ask us to give up the buffalo for the sheep. The
young men have heard talk of this and it has made them sad
and angry. Do not speak of it more.[33]

But they did. The commissioners made it clear that the
Great Father could also be a harsh parent. If his red children
balked, he would send soldiers to punish them. Surely, they
remembered the Second Cavalry. It no longer existed, but other
regiments could take its place. They had fought in the big palefaces' war and had defeated even the Texans.

Such straight talk persuaded ten Comanche chiefs to put
their mark on the treaty. They hated doing so. But at least it gave
them a place free from white invaders, and guaranteed their right
to hunt the buffalo. After the signing, the Comanche returned
the visitors' hospitality with a dog feast. Their guests did their
part; they ate up, politely, if not enthusiastically.[34]

The Treaty of Medicine Lodge was doomed from the outset.
Both sides were at fault. White racism, the idea that certain peoples are naturally inferior to others, played an important role in the
treaty's failure. Racism was (and is) widespread in the United

States. One of the arguments for slavery had been that black people, being inferior, must work for their white "betters"; indeed, it was for their own benefit, a kind of training in responsibility. The same applied to Native Americans. The basic idea was that whites knew better than Indians what was good for them. White leaders regarded Indians as overgrown children, whose way of life deserved no respect and whose wishes needed to be honored only when convenient. Treaties were constantly being made, and broken; for the aim was always to increase control of the tribes until whites could act without regard to the Indians' wishes. In short, treaties were made to be broken at a future time, when convenient. Even had the author-

ities been sincere, they could not have enforced the treaties. The United States really is a democracy, and democracy is government by the people through their elected representatives. Unpopular treaties could not be enforced without the people's consent. Any treaty that gave the Indians territory would have to be broken when enough white voters set their sights on the same land.

In signing the Treaty of Medicine Lodge, the chiefs acted only for themselves. They could not even force their own bands to obey; warriors could still go raiding if they could get others to follow them. Besides, only the Yamparika, Penateka, and Nokoni had attended the council. The Quahadi and Kotsoteka stayed away, preferring to hunt rather than to talk. The Quahadi had never met the cavalry in battle; in fact, no cavalry had ever ventured onto the Staked Plain. "Toothless old squaws" might sign treaties, but the Quahadi meant to fight.

Ten Bears of the Yamparika Comanche spoke eloquently at Medicine Lodge, saying that his people wanted to live freely in their own land and not copy the ways of the whites.

Ten Bears probably had little faith in the treaty. Why else would he say his young men were sad and angry? He knew his people. War and war honors stood at the center of Comanche life. Theirs was a society built on war. A young man could earn no respect until he became a warrior. Without war honors to his credit, no girl would have him as a husband. Without war honors, braves, and even small children, would make fun of him. Thus, the Treaty of Medicine Lodge kept the younger generation from growing up. And that was intolerable.

Certainly Quanah Parker had no intention of being bound by ink stains on a scrap of paper. When the council broke up, he went to Quina-bivi and Horse's Back, veteran Nokoni war chiefs, like his father. "You have taken your scalps, and won honor as warriors," he said bitterly. "You have many ponies, and it pleases you to have the gifts and rations of the white men. But you are taking away the chance of the young men. We, too, want to win honors."[35]

He had grown to manhood among the Nokoni. But now he must leave. He would ride west, to the Staked Plain and the Quahadi. "The Quahadis are free," he said. "I am going to them, and we shall live just as we have always lived. Tell the white chiefs, when they ask, that the Quahadi are warriors and that we are not afraid."[36]

Quanah Parker's interesting times had only just begun.

Bad Hand Mackenzie

"Mackenzie, you have been ordered down here . . . because . . . I want you to *control* and *hold down* the situation, and to *do it in your own way.* I want you to be bold, enterprising, and at all times *full of energy.* When you begin, let it be a campaign of *annihilation, obliteration* and *complete destruction,* as you have always in your dealings done to all the Indians you have dealt with."

—General Philip H. Sheridan to Colonel Ranald S. Mackenzie

QUANAH Parker won many war honors with the Quahadi. In the year after Medicine Lodge, he seemed always to be on the warpath. He rode with war parties into Mexico, raided the Navajo in New Mexico, and fought the *Tejanos* at every opportunity.

During a raid along the Pease River, near where his mother had been captured, a cavalry patrol attacked his war party, killing Bear Claw, its leader. Quanah's comrades panicked, thinking themselves deserted by their guardian spirits. Not the son of Peta Nocona.

"Spread out!" Quanah shouted. "Do not all keep together. Turn the horses north to the river."[1]

There was such authority in his voice that they pulled themselves together immediately. Here was a natural leader! Here was someone who could inspire others, because his medicine was so strong!

Quanah dropped back to cover their escape. Just then, one of the troopers raced ahead of the others, firing as he came. A bullet whooshed past Quanah's head, then

Quanah Parker about the year 1880. By this time he had taken a leading role in guiding his people's relations with the white authorities at Fort Sill, Oklahoma.

another, but he kept calm. Circling a clump of bushes, he dropped over the side of his horse and aimed at the soldier. *Thump!* An arrow struck the man's shoulder, making him drop his weapon and turn back.

The other soldiers hesitated for a moment, then continued their charge with six-shooters blazing. Quanah wheeled his horse around and raced after his friends, who had used the moments he bought them to reach the far bank. Now it was Quanah's turn. Man and horse plunged into the river and swam to safety, leaving their pursuers behind. When the braves camped that night, they chose Quanah as their leader. Quanah Parker, at twenty-three, was a war chief. Within four years, he would be the principal war chief of the Quahadi.

In Quanah's many battles with whites, no one ever accused him of cruelty. He had been born a Comanche, raised a Comanche, and was a Comanche through and through. Yet for some reason, still unclear, he broke with the Comanche practice of mistreating captives. Charles Goodnight, a former Texas Ranger and a leading rancher, later became his friend. Goodnight declared that the chief "never allowed any woman to be killed," let alone tortured.[2]

He had no qualms about killing white men, but here, too, he showed mercy. Take the two cavalrymen captured during a raid in Texas. Having heard tales of Comanche "savagery," they expected the worst. Quanah, however, said they would not be harmed unless they tried to escape. One fellow pretended to be content, but after a few days his companion asked to be released. Quanah promised to let him go if he ran down a double line of warriors, one warrior standing every ten feet with a bow and one arrow. He never made it.[3]

The other fellow eventually escaped, thanks to advice from one of the chief's wives. Why she offered this advice is a mystery; but the fact that she did shows that not all squaws tortured prisoners. In any case, she told him to say he intended to spend the rest of his life with the Quahadi. If invited to go hunting, he was to welcome the chance, but get "lost" on the way back to camp. Searchers would be sent out, only to find him heading toward the camp. He was to repeat this several times, always arriving an hour or so after the others. When the hunters got used to his lateness, he was to ride toward the rising sun, back to the Texas settlements.[4]

As Quanah's fame spread, braves left the reservation and headed for the Staked Plain. They yearned for the free life and the thrills of the warpath; most of all, they resented white domination. The reservation, to them, was a prison, a place that robbed them of their manhood. Others, equally warlike, became "reservation jumpers." But rather than leave permanently, they used the reservation as a base of operations. Since it was so large, war parties could easily slip across the Red River into Texas. Usually they made their way on foot to avoid detection. Once across the river, they stole horses from ranches and set to work. After a few weeks of raiding, they returned to collect their government rations.

Washington bureaucrats were often ignorant of frontier realities. They had never seen a Plains Indian, let alone studied the role of war in his society. The Office of Indian Affairs, joined by well-intentioned easterners, insisted that kindness produces kindness and that braves would respond to fair treatment and appeals to their better nature. This was a very simple view of things. Indians *had* been treated badly, but that did not mean whites were always the aggressors. Many tribes like the Comanche lived for battle. Moreover, those who branded soldiers as "butchers, sots determined to exterminate the noble redman, and foment wars so that they had employment," were just plain wrong.[5] Crazy as it seems, officials gave warriors guns and ammunition, including repeating rifles, even though federal law prohibited their sale to Indians. The reason, they said, was the tribes' lack of weapons for "hunting."[6]

By 1871, the Texas frontier was suffering as in the worst days of the Civil War. The Treaty of Medicine Lodge prevented angry

Texans from crossing into the Indian Territory. Once a posse chased raiders across the Red River. The braves halted on the northern bank, shouting insults at the frustrated *Tejanos*. And, as usual, women and children were kidnapped; indeed, some were held in camps within sight of Fort Sill. Soldiers saw them, but were forbidden to interfere. The kidnappers, however, interpreted lack of action as weakness. One white girl, ransomed after a winter of abuse, had learned Comanche. She heard squaws boasting about "the fine things those damned fools, the *Americanos*, would give their men for a few *Tejano* rats" like herself.[7] Even if a brave waved bloody scalps in front of the fort commander, he could not be arrested for crimes committed outside the reservation.

Texans were furious. Protesters demanded protection. Newspapers thundered against government "cowardice or imbecility."[8] The frontier would never know peace "until the Indians are all killed off, or until they are caught and caged."[9] Something had to be done, and quickly, or the Texas plains would be abandoned by whites.

Government officials, safe behind their desks, said the Texans were exaggerating. General Sherman, a six-footer with flaming red hair and a temper to match, was not so sure. As the army's general in chief, he decided to find out for himself. Early in May 1871, he left San Antonio in an army ambulance fixed up as a traveling coach, escorted by fifteen cavalrymen. The blackened chimneys and freshly dug graves he saw proved that the Texans were not exaggerating.

Sherman almost filled one of those graves himself. As his caravan moved westward, over a hundred Kiowa braves left the Fort Sill reservation. They were led by three famous war chiefs—Satanta, Satank (Sitting Bear), and A'do-eete (Big Tree)—and the medicine man Dohate (Owl Prophet.) On the night of May 17, the war party camped near Salt Creek Prairie south of Fort Richardson. Dohate had fallen asleep after making his medicine. It must have been strong medicine, since an owl spirit came to him in a dream. It told him that two groups of whites would cross

Satank was Satanta's accomplice in the massacre of the army wagon drivers. He was shot trying to escape while being taken to Texas to face charges of murder.

the prairie next day. The warriors should let the first group pass in safety, but the second must be wiped out.

Warriors watched from their hiding places as Sherman's party rode by, unaware that their lives had been saved by a dream-owl. An hour later, ten army supply wagons rolled across the prairie. Seven out of the ten drivers were killed and their bodies mutilated. One poor fellow was chained to a wheel upside down and a fire built under his face. It was a low fire, so he died slowly.

Moments after Sherman arrived at Fort Richardson, one of the drivers stumbled through the gate. Though in a state of shock, he told of his escape and of the "Wagon Train Massacre." Instantly, the general ordered a cavalry patrol to visit the scene of the massacre, identify the raiders if possible, and report to him at Fort Sill, his next stop.

The raiders reached the reservation the same day as Sherman. No one would have been the wiser had Satanta not bragged about the killings. Yet he did, probably in the belief that the general was bound by the same rules as the fort's commander. Sherman, however, was not only head of the army, but a friend of President Ulysses S. Grant. During the Civil War, Grant and Sherman had been an unbeatable team, winning key victories against the Confederates. Sherman knew that Grant would back him all the way.

Next day, Sherman arrested the three Kiowa chiefs and sent them to Texas for trial. Satank was a proud man, a Koh-eet-senko, one of his people's ten greatest warriors. He did not see himself as a criminal, and had no intention of being humiliated in a *Tejano* courtroom. Death, for Satank, was better than dishonor. When they were a few miles from Fort Sill, he worked his hands free from the handcuffs and began to sing his death song:

render, most of that magnificent force had been disbanded. The world's largest war machine shrank from over one million men to a mere twenty-five thousand. Nearly every officer had to accept a lower rank at lower pay or leave the service. Major generals became colonels, colonels majors or captains, and so on down the chain of command. Some officers, indeed, stepped back into the ranks, becoming sergeants or even corporals. Promotion was so slow that men retired as first lieutenants after spending thirty years in uniform. Though bitter and frustrated over their careers, they gave the army an officer corps that was second to none. All were experienced fighters of proven ability.

Most enlisted men were happy to return to their families. Civilian life, however, did not appeal to everyone. Sometimes their jobs were gone, or their girls had married others. Some just found peace dull after the excitement of battle. The army had gotten into their blood, had become a part of them, drawing them back like a magnet. Others, too young for the Civil War, wanted to see what they had missed. They were men like Private Jacob Adams, who enlisted because he "fairly ached to get into some action like that I had heard veterans of the Civil War talk about."[12]

The army was a cross section of America. Men of every race, religion, and walk of life served in its ranks. They were joined by immigrants from Ireland, England, Germany, France, Italy, Holland, and Russia. Many spoke little English, irritating their officers no end. As a soldier-poet observed:

> Maginnis scowls at Johnny Bull, an' Yawcob
> > Meyer roars
> At Jean Duval; an' I have heard the
> > comp'ny countin' fours
> In seven different languages; on which
> > eventful day
> The captain burst a blood vessel, an'
> > fainted dead away.[13]

Former Confederates also enlisted. After the Civil War, thousands of "Johnny Rebs" found nothing worth returning to in the South. Some left the country to serve in foreign armies; others set out to fight Indians. So did thousands of blacks, discharged Union soldiers and ex-slaves who went West in search of opportunity. Four black regiments—the Ninth and Tenth cavalries and the Twenty-fourth and Twenty-fifth infantries—were posted on the frontier. Several companies of black cavalrymen were stationed at Fort Sill. It was they who arrested the Kiowa chiefs.

Indians had mixed feelings about blacks. On the one hand, they respected them as fighters, calling them Buffalo Soldiers because they had curly, kinky hair like the buffalo's. But they also regarded them as demons. "We thought these Negroes came from under the water, from the fact that our shadow always appeared black in water," recalled Herman Lehman, a white boy adopted by the Comanches. "I remember hearing our chief instruct his warriors, at one time, that in fighting the buffalo soldiers never shoot them in the head. He said: 'Skull too hard; turn arrows, mash bullets, break spears, dull lances. Shoot him

Members of the Sixth U.S. Cavalry Regiment in training. Cavalry horses were taught to lie down to provide cover for their riders on the open plains.

through heart; kill him easy.'"[14] This advice was nonsense; shoot anyone in the head and he goes down.

The cavalry was the army's main striking force. A cavalryman wore a blue uniform with a yellow stripe along the seams of his pants, a slouch hat, high boots, and a bandanna knotted around the neck. The bandanna had many uses. Tied as a tourniquet, it stopped bleeding; worn over the face as a mask, it kept out the dust. Cavalry weapons were a fifteen-shot rifle weighing ten pounds and a Colt Army .44 revolver weighing three pounds. The army version of the Colt was fourteen inches long, so the trooper could use it as a club when empty and the enemy was within arm's reach. The saber, a curved steel blade three feet long and weighing five pounds, looked nice on parade but was useless against a Comanche lance. Despite movie westerns, troopers left their sabers behind, or "lost" them soon after setting out on patrol.

A regiment was based at several forts. Plains forts were simple affairs. Since timber was scarce, forts were usually not surrounded by log walls. Instead, rows of buildings were arranged in a square around a parade ground. On one side were the single-men's barracks, long, two-story structures with overhanging roofs to give shade. Across the way was "sudsville," where married soldiers lived and their wives did the laundry. The rest of the square was taken up by officers' houses, headquarters, mess hall, hospital, storehouses, and blacksmith's shop. Behind these were the stables, corrals, and latrines.

Living in a fort was neither pleasant nor glamorous. The odors of sweat, manure, and gun oil hung in the air. Packs of dogs set up a howl whenever a bugle sounded. Unmarried men slept two to a bunk, on a "hay bag" filled with straw; hay that was not changed frequently became infested with fleas, hence the name "fleabag." Each soldier had one blanket, which he shared with his "bunkie." Barracks, a veteran recalled, were "filled with bedbugs, fleas, rats, mice, etc." In addition, there were scorpions and tarantulas, large, hairy spiders the size of a man's fist. Soldiers slept on

Fort Sill, Indian Territory, later the state of Oklahoma, in 1871. Unlike forts in the eastern woodlands, those on the Great Plains were not surrounded by log palisades. For defense, the buildings were arranged in a large square protected by cannons and Gatling guns, an early type of machine gun. No Great Plains fort was ever taken by Indians.

the parade ground during the summer to avoid being eaten alive by these pests.[15]

Keeping clean was nearly impossible, since barracks were not equipped with bathtubs. Soldiers might spend their entire career in a fort without once taking a bath. Or, for that matter, eating a nutritious meal. The ration—one day's food supply for one man—consisted of beef hash, hard bread, and coffee for breakfast; salt pork, bread, and coffee for lunch; bread and coffee for supper. The salt pork was called "salt horse," because horseshoes were said to be found at the bottom of the barrels in which it came. There was no milk, butter, eggs, or fruit. Vegetables might be grown in private gardens, if the grasshoppers weren't too bad. An officer explained: "The damn hoppers came along, by God, and ate my garden, by God, then the birds ate the hoppers, by God, and we killed and ate the birds, by God, so that we were even in the long run."[16]

Nothing compared to the Texas climate, except the climate of Arizona. Soldiers looked forward to summer with dread. Heat waves shimmered on the Plains at midday, making them "dance." The dry heat cracked your lips and blistered your nose. Streams

ran dry, and water had to be rationed, often to a cup a day. Horses got special treatment, for a cavalryman was nothing without his mount. If necessary, he was expected to give his last drop of water to his horse. Men on patrol fought off sunstroke by placing wet rags in the crowns of their hats.

Texas was compared to hell, to the advantage of hell. Men told of an imaginary comrade who died and went below, only to return for his blanket. A popular poem had the title "How the Devil Located a Claim in Texas for a New Hell." Satan, it seems, wanted to move. Dissatisfied with the old, cozy hell, he asked God to give him a hotter, drier, nastier hell. The Lord told him to have a look at Texas; if he liked it, it was his. He found it perfect.

Officers' quarters at a western fort. As the picture shows, life in a frontier outpost was not luxurious.

And the devil then said: 'I have all that is needed
To make a good hell,' and hence he succeeded.
He began to put thorns on all the trees,
And mix up the sand with millions of fleas;
And scattered tarantulas along all the roads;
Put thorns on the cactus and horns on the toads.
He lengthened the horns on the Texas steers,
And put additions to the rabbits' ears;
He put a little devil in the bronco steed
And poisoned the feet of the centipede.
The rattlesnake bites you, the scorpion stings,
The mosquito delights you with buzzing wings;
The sandburs prevail and so do the ants,
And those who sit down need half-soles on their
    pants.
The heat in the summer is a hundred and ten,
Too hot for the devil and too hot for men,
The black boar roams through the black
    chaparral,
It is a hell of a place he has for a hell.[17]

Every waking hour was governed by the bugle. The trooper's day began with reveille at 5:30 A.M. and ended with taps at 10:00 P.M. In between, he "policed" his barracks, looked after his horse, cleaned his weapons, stood for inspections, and worked on various post projects known as "fatigues": repairing buildings, digging wells, mapping the countryside, stringing telegraph wire. For this he received thirteen dollars a month, raised to sixteen after five years of service. Yet, apart from gambling and cheap liquor, he had little use for money "in the middle of nowhere." Bored and depressed, he went on drunken binges, for which he spent time in the guardhouse on bread and water. Often he ran away; between 1867 and 1891, a third of all recruits deserted. Some men cracked up entirely; on average, seventy-six out of every thousand soldiers committed suicide each year.[18]

Married men seemed to be more content than bachelors. Army wives *were* special. It took a strong, loving woman to put up with life in a frontier fort. Not only did she have to adjust to harsh living conditions, she knew what to expect if captured by Indians. She was taught to ride and shoot as soon as possible, if she did not already know how. She was also taught that she must never, *ever*, show fear of Indians. If she met Indians in or near the fort, she must move slowly, speak softly, and be calm. One rule was drummed into her head: Never be taken alive.

Lieutenant John W. Summerhays, Eighth Infantry, was a typical husband in this respect. His wife and baby were in a wagon train he was escorting when Comanches struck. During the fight, he galloped back to the ambulance in which they were riding. "Now listen," he told his wife grimly, "if I'm hit, you'll know what to do. You have your [pistol], and when you see there is no help for it . . . why there's only one thing to be done. Don't let them get the baby, for they will carry you both off and well, you know the squaws are much crueler than the bucks. *Don't let them get either of you alive.*"[19] If a husband doubted his wife's determination, he might ask a friend to shoot his loved ones in case he

Off duty. A group of officers pose with their families at a fort somewhere on the Great Plains. Army wives were strong women, able to ride and shoot.

was not there. Colonel George Armstrong Custer, Seventh Cavalry, had a standing order for his aides to shoot his wife, Elizabeth, rather than let Indians take her. Soldiers so feared capture that they had a motto: "Always save the last bullet for yourself." When Custer was overrun by the Sioux in 1876, several troopers blew their brains out at the last moment.

× × ×

General Sheridan turned his attention to the Quahadi. Beat the Quahadi, he reasoned, and you beat The People as a whole. Quanah Parker's band had challenged the army to come and get them on the Staked Plain. Very well, it would do just that. Their defeat would not only clear the Staked Plain but convince the Comanche of the hopelessness of further resistance. Discouraged, they would resign themselves to life on the reservation.

The task was given to Ranald S. Mackenzie, probably the best Indian fighter the army ever produced. Not only would Mackenzie humble the Comanche, he would go on to victories against the Sioux, Cheyenne, and Apache. A no-nonsense soldier, he had entered the Union army immediately upon graduating West Point in 1862. In less than three years, he rose from a second lieutenant to a major general in command of a cavalry corps. Ulysses S. Grant, a good judge of fighting men, called him "the most promising young officer in the army." Yet it was a miracle that he survived. Always in the thick of the fight, he was wounded six times. In one battle, his horse was cut in two by a shell and he was nearly killed. But he refused to leave the battlefield. Two fingers of his right hand were shot off during another battle. This inspired the Indians to call him Bad Hand or Threefingers.

Bad Hand Mackenzie loved the army. With him, duty came first, last, and always. Apart from soldiering, he had no private life (he was a bachelor) and no interests. A cold, distant man, he seldom smiled and never laughed out loud; mostly, he scowled and "chewed out" anyone who displeased him. Reduced in rank after the Civil War, he became colonel of the Fourth Cavalry, a crack outfit that had been in seventy-six battles against the Confederates. Now it would face Quanah Parker and the Quahadi. Its commander's aim was simple, and brutal. All Comanches would be "dismounted, disarmed and made to raise corn."[20] No more raiding and hunting for them! They would be swept from the Plains, or be turned into buzzard bait.

During the summer of 1871, the Fourth Cavalry concentrated at Fort Richardson. From there, Mackenzie sent patrols to probe the canyons along the eastern fringes of the Staked Plain. Veteran troopers from the East, who thought they had seen it all, were in for a shock. If Virginia in summer was hot, West Texas was "hell with the lid off." Every day was a scorcher. Sunglasses had yet to be invented, so the bright light made their eyes ache. The food was awful. Field rations consisted of fatty bacon crusted with salt, hard biscuits, and coffee. Water, when available, was found in stagnant pools covered with a green scum. This evil stuff was boiled for coffee and served "hot as hell and black as sin" to mask the taste. Quanah's people, of course, knew every stream on the Staked Plain. In times of scarcity, they chewed cactus pulp for moisture. If things really got bad, they opened a vein in their horses' necks and lapped the blood.

Bad Hand led his regiment into enemy territory early in the fall. On the evening of October 9, he camped along the Fresh Water Fork of the Brazos River, near where it breaks out of the Staked Plain through Blanco Canyon. The Quahadi were near; that he knew, thanks to his Tonkawa scouts, who had been reading their "sign" for several days. What he did not know was that he was about to begin a four-day contest with their chief.

It was a peaceful night. All was still, save for the rustling of horses and the footsteps of sentries walking their posts. Their comrades, exhausted and dust-covered from a day in the saddle,

Known to the Indians as "Bad Hand," due to a Civil War wound, Colonel Ranald Mackenzie routed the Comanches in the Palo Duro Canyon of Texas.

slept on waterproof sheets covered by blankets. Always cautious, Bad Hand had forbidden campfires. The only light came from above, where a full moon hung like a lantern in the black sky.

Mackenzie was right to be careful. This was unknown country; none of the intruders, whites or Tonkawas, had ever come so close to the Staked Plain. But Quanah's scouts knew every inch of it and had been watching the colonel's every movement.

Around midnight, Quanah struck without warning. He came not to fight, since Comanches feared being killed in the darkness, but to drive off the cavalry's horses. And drive them off he did! The chief led his braves through the camp, firing six-shooters, yelling, ringing cowbells, and dragging buffalo hides at the end of lariats. It was pandemonium.

Horses reared and plunged, pulling out the iron picket pins that fastened their bridle ropes to the ground. Picket pins whizzed through the darkness, past men's heads, deadly as bullets. "Get to your horses!" officers shouted, scrambling to their feet. "Every man to his lariat!"

It was too late. Within seconds, Quanah's men had escaped with seventy of the regiment's best horses, including the colonel's favorite mount. Quanah named him Running Deer and rode him with pride. Later, in defeat, he offered to return the horse. Bad Hand refused; Quanah had won it fair and square, and he was no sore loser.[21]

Early next morning, October 10, a twelve-man patrol went in search of the missing horses. It was led by Captain Edward M. Heyl and Lieutenant Robert G. Carter. The lieutenant was more than a brave soldier; he was a talented writer with a gift for putting his readers right into the action. His book, *On the Border with Mackenzie, or the Winning of West Texas from the Comanches*, is the best eyewitness account of Bad Hand's campaigns. It has become a classic in Western Americana.

The patrol saw a small group of Quahadi driving horses two miles from camp. They seemed surprised at the patrol's appearance. Abandoning the horses, they plunged into a ravine and rode out on the other side, heading for a hill near the mouth of Blanco Canyon. The troopers sped after them, steadily closing the distance. Reaching the top of the hill, they suddenly reined in their mounts. The "fleeing" braves had led them into an ambush. There, coming on at a full gallop, was a swarm of warriors led by Quanah Parker. "Heavens, but we are in a nest!" Heyl cried. "Just look at the Indians!"[22]

Carter's mind raced. The obvious course was to get back to the ravine without delay. But their horses were winded and would probably give out before they reached safety. Besides, no one in his right mind would show his back to Comanches pursuing on fresh mounts. The troopers' only chance was to dismount and slowly back up toward the ravine. Their rifles might—just might—win them a few extra minutes by slowing the attack. And if Bad Hand heard the shooting, he would send the regiment to the rescue. If not, well, boys, save the last bullet for yourselves!

Carter turned to Heyl, who was riding on his right. He was shocked at what he saw. The captain's face was white as a sheet. Paralyzed with fear, he gave no orders, but stared blankly into space. The lieutenant shouted his plan, which Heyl agreed to by nodding his head. Carter barked an order for the troopers to dismount, form two firing parties, and back up slowly. It worked! A hail of rifle bullets caused the braves to slow their charge, if only for a moment.

That moment allowed Carter to take a mental snapshot of the scene. The picture burned itself into his memory. He wrote:

> The well delivered fire of our little handful of men . . . caused the savages to falter and hesitate, and to commence their curious custom of circling. They were naked to the waist; were arrayed in all their war paint and trinkets, with head dresses or war bonnets of fur or feathers fantastically ornamented. Their ponies . . . were striped and otherwise artistically painted and decorated with gaudy strips of flannel and

All in a day's work. Artist Charles Schrevogel shows a skirmish between Indians and cavalrymen in one of his paintings of army life on the Plains. Fearing torture if captured, many cavalrymen saved their last bullet for themselves.

calico. Bells were jingling, feathers waving, and with jubilant, discordant yells that would have put a blush to any Confederate brigade of the Civil War, and uttering taunting shouts, they pressed on. . . . Mingled with the shouts, whoops and yells of the warriors could be distinctly heard the strident screeching and higher-keyed piercing screams of the squaws, far in the rear of the moving circles, which rose above the general din. . . . In the midst of the circling ponies we could see . . . two scalp poles gaily decorated with long scalp locks, probably of women, with feathers and pieces of bright metal attached which flashed in the morning light. There were also other flashes seen along their line which I afterwards ascertained were small pieces of mirrors held in the hand and used as signals. . . . [23]

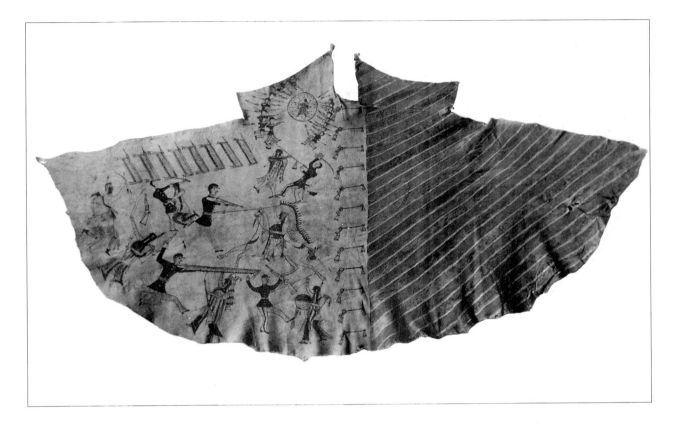

A shout from a trooper at his side distracted Carter. "Lieutenant, look over there, quick; they are running out!"[24] It was true. Heyl and his seven men had remounted and were galloping away. Carter and his men yelled pleas and curses, but they kept going. The lieutenant heard Comanches yell, too—in happiness—as they turned the full weight of their attack against him and his five men.

Carter had no choice. Ordering his men to remount, he told them to bend low on their horses and turn to fire single shots as they rode toward the ravine. The lieutenant's cool courage held his men together—he would win the Congressional Medal of Honor for his leadership this day.

Slowly, yard by yard, they fell back. As they neared the ravine, Carter shouted: "Now, men . . . bunch your shots, pump it into them, and make a dash for your lives! It is all we can do!"[25] Again a hail of bullets sent the Quahadis reeling. The troopers

A tipi cover with a painting of a battle scene between Kiowa braves and cavalrymen. Such scenes were like posters indicating that the owner was a worthy man deserving of respect.

sprang forward, but Private Seander Gregg, who had been riding just behind Carter, never reached the destination.

"Lieutenant," he cried, "my horse is giving out!"[26] Sure enough, the animal was swaying, totally exhausted. Quanah saw this, too, and came like a whirlwind. Carter could not take his eyes off the chief:

A large and powerfully built chief led the bunch, on a coal-black racing pony. Leaning forward upon his mane, his heels nervously working in the animal's side, with six-shooter poised in the air, he seemed the incarnation of savage brutal joy. His face was smeared with black war paint, which gave his features a satanic look. A large, cruel mouth added to his ferocious appearance. A full-length headdress or war bonnet of eagle's feathers, spreading out as he rode, and descending from his forehead, over head and back, to his pony's tail, almost swept the ground. Large brass hoops were in his ears; he was naked to his waist, wearing simply leggings, moccasins and a breechclout. A necklace of bear's claws hung about his neck. His scalp lock was carefully braided in with otter fur, and tied with bright red flannel. His horse's bridle was profusely ornamented with bits of silver, and red flannel was also braided into his mane and tail, but, being black, he was not painted. Bells jingled as he rode at headlong speed, followed by the leading warriors, all eager to outstrip him in the race.[27]

But they could not keep up with Quanah. Private Gregg was doomed, and the chief meant to be his executioner. "Pull your six-shooter!" Carter called over his shoulder. Too late! As Gregg reached for his weapon, Quanah's own six-shooter flamed at the back of his head. Down he went. His horse, relieved of Gregg's weight, turned and ran toward the Indians.[28]

Without pausing to scalp his victim, Quanah whirled and sped away at the head of his braves. Moments later, Carter learned why. Quanah's keen eyes had seen a cloud of dust in the distance. Rising dust meant either a sandstorm or a body of horsemen coming fast. Sure enough, scores of troopers appeared moments later. Bad Hand had heard the shooting and sent them to the rescue. There were no bugle calls, as in a movie rescue; real troopers did not warn the enemy of their approach. At the ravine, Carter and his men, having thought themselves goners, breathed a sigh of relief.

Next day, October 11, the Fourth Cavalry set out after the Quahadi. It was rough going. Not only were they in strange country, Quanah led them on a wild-goose chase through Blanco Canyon. To confuse the pursuers, he divided his band into two groups, having them cross and recross each other's trails. For the first time, the Tonkawas were puzzled. After much debate, they decided that the wily chief had doubled back to his original camp-site. Mackenzie followed, only to find that Quanah had doubled back yet again. This time he had taken a steep trail up the wall of the canyon and gone over the rim, onto the Staked Plain.

Bad Hand followed on October 12. What a sight! Coming over the rim, the Fourth Cavalry stood on the Staked Plain. Flat as a board, it seemed to go on forever. "As far as the eye could reach," Carter recalled, "not a bush or tree, a twig or stone, not an object of any kind or a living thing, was in sight. It stretched out before us—one uninterrupted plain, only to be compared to the ocean in vastness."[29] Pointing westward was a fresh trail made by at least a thousand horses. The parallel marks of travois poles, loaded with household goods and dragged on either side of the squaws' horses, were a sure sign that the Quahadi were up ahead.

Mackenzie stood in his stirrups and pointed west. The Fourth Cavalry went forward. Each company followed its own guidon, a fork-tailed flag used for identification. Victory was near. They could feel it in their bones.

Troopers pushed themselves and their mounts without mercy. Before long, they sighted Quanah's people far in the distance. The chief saw them, too. With the troopers gaining on them, he and his braves dropped back from the caravan. Placing them on either side of Mackenzie's column, he aimed to lure him into a fight, thus giving the women and children time to escape. But the colonel refused the bait. He went straight for the main body.

Gradually, the cavalry closed the distance. They would have gone all the way, had a norther not struck without warning at the last moment. Wind whistled across the plain, bringing snow and sleet. The Staked Plain is more than three thousand feet above sea level. Mackenzie's troopers had spent months on the hot Plains hundreds of feet lower in elevation. They still wore summer uniforms, and were unprepared for the sudden drop in temperature. With his men chilled to the bone, and the Quahadi hidden by the storm, the colonel called a halt.

When the norther passed, the Quahadi were gone. Quanah had not stopped for the storm. He had used the opportunity to return to Blanco Canyon, then climb back onto the Staked Plain a second time. Mackenzie, however, was no quitter. He kept after the Quahadi, driving his men to the limits of their endurance. Keeping up became a matter of soldierly pride. "We consoled ourselves," Carter recalled, "with the thought that if Indians with their women and children could endure it, we certainly must."[30]

Mackenzie's determination brought them to within a mile of the fleeing band. But as darkness came on, another norther struck, causing the Quahadi to vanish as if a black curtain had dropped behind them. This time the storm raged for hours. Bad Hand had to give up the chase until daylight.

Troopers swore this was the worst night of their lives; nothing they had gone through in the Civil War compared to it. Egg-size hailstones fell, pelting men and horses. Their clothes frozen to their skin, men huddled under blankets, trying to share body heat. Mackenzie probably suffered most. Someone put a buffalo robe over his shoulders, but it did not keep out the cold. His shivered through the night, tormented by his old wounds.

October 13 dawned bright and cold. By then, however, the

Quahadi were long gone. Quanah had kept them moving throughout the night. The only sign of the fleeing band was a trail of discarded camp equipment: tipi covers, tipi poles, bundles of firewood, stone mortars and pestles. Scores of puppies had also been left behind, which troopers adopted as mascots. Still, they were in no condition to keep up the chase. With their horses giving out, and rations running low, Mackenzie decided to return to Fort Richardson. Having made his decision, his men avoided him unless absolutely necessary. They knew the colonel's moods. Angry with himself for failing, he was fit company only for rattlesnakes.

The return to Blanco Canyon did not improve his temper. As the column came down the trail, two Quahadi scouts were discovered leading their horses up on foot. They were promptly shot, but not before one sent a barbed arrow into Mackenzie's leg. The arrow was removed intact, but he had to spend a few weeks on crutches. Once, when an aide spoke out of turn, Bad Hand whacked him over the head with a crutch.

The scouts suffered a fate worse than death, for a Comanche. What happened next would cripple them for eternity and prove that not all "savages" wore war paint. The regimental surgeon, Dr. Rufus Choate, cut off their heads and brought them to camp in a canvas sack. He planned to donate them to a museum or to a medical school for study.

That night, Dr. Choate's assistant invited Lieutenant Carter and a friend for supper. "Come up," he said cheerfully, "we have something good!"

They found two large kettles hung on a pole over a fire—the same kettles in which the regiment's meals were cooked. The guests took their cups, eager for a taste of hot "soup." But it was just a sick joke. Leaning over the kettle, "we saw two Comanche scalped heads, with the stripes of paint still on their faces, and with eyes partly opened, bobbing up and down, and rising above the mess kettles, mingled with the bubbling, bloody broth." Carter and his friend grabbed their stomachs and ran. "We were no longer hungry that night."[31]

The Fourth Cavalry had not done well. Its colonel was the first to admit that fact. "We didn't look worth a damn," he said when the troops returned to base.[32] They had marched over five hundred miles and lost only one man, but they had lost dozens of horses. They had killed a handful of braves, but did no more than give the Quahadi a scare. Still, the campaign taught Mackenzie a great deal about the Comanche and their methods of fighting. He had also taken the measure of their young war chief, Quanah Parker. Next year, he vowed, his knowledge would be put to good use.

Luck was with him. In March 1872, a patrol caught up to a small war party, killing two braves and capturing a Mexican boy. That boy proved to be worth his weight in gold. Upon questioning, he admitted to working for the Comancheros. More, he said there was a wagon road across the Staked Plain, over which stolen cattle were driven from Texas to New Mexico. Bad Hand was thrilled. With the boy showing the way, he found the road and followed it clear into New Mexico. Then, turning southeastward, he found yet another road, which led to Tule Canyon. This *was* something to cheer about! In thirty days he had marched 640 miles and worn the shoes off nearly every horse in his command. But he had exploded the myth that soldiers could not operate on the Staked Plain. He could now strike deep into the Quahadi homeland.

Mackenzie took the offensive in the fall. On September 29, Tonkawa scouts located a large camp on the North Fork of the Red River. It was the camp of Quanah's ally, Mow-Way (Handshaker), a Kotsoteka war chief. Mow-Way's people, unaware of the danger, were busy tanning buffalo hides and making pemmican. Nearly all the warriors were away on a buffalo hunt.

The Fourth Cavalry came like a whirlwind. The few remaining warriors escaped, but the women and children were too slow. The troopers captured 127 of them and some 900 horses. A white prisoner held in the camp was ashamed of his people. The troopers, he said, "tried to make a massacre of this attack, for they killed many squaws, babies, warriors, and old white headed men."[33] Mackenzie claimed that the innocents had been killed accidentally, in the crossfire. Fifty Kotsoteka died; four troopers lost their lives. The entire camp of 262 lodges was burned to ashes. The Comanche had their first taste of total war.

The braves, however, did not give up easily. That night, they returned with a vengeance. Firing guns and ringing cowbells, they ran off the captured horses, while many prisoners escaped in the confusion. It was a setback for Mackenzie, and he swore terribly. But his anger quickly cooled. Despite the setback, he had proven that he could find and fight the Comanche in their own country. A week later, some Quahadi who had been camped near Mow-Way went to the reservation. No place, they explained, was safe from the three-fingered one.

Mackenzie intended to go after Quanah next summer. But the chief got an unexpected break, thanks to the Kickapoo. This tribe had once lived north of the Red River. During the Civil War, it migrated to Mexico and began raiding Texas from across the Rio Grande. Pursued by cavalry, the raiders would return to their Mexican sanctuary. Amercan complaints had no effect; Mexican authorities insisted the Kickapoo were a peaceful people who helped defend against the Comanches.

During the spring of 1873, General Sheridan and Colonel Mackenzie met secretly. Sheridan announced that President Grant had lost patience with the Kickapoo. The Fourth Cavalry must go into Mexico and teach them a bloody lesson. Yes, taking troops onto foreign soil was an invasion, an act of war. The president, of course, had no intention of fighting Mexico over a few Indians. That was why Mackenzie could not have written orders. "Damn the orders!" cried Sheridan when he asked for them.[34] Bad Hand was to go on his own initiative, and take the blame if anything went wrong. *That* was an order. And so Mackenzie crossed the Rio Grande on May 17, galloped seventy-six miles in sweltering heat, and destroyed three Kickapoo villages. He returned the next day, having lost only one man. The Mexican government protested, but President Grant backed his favorite officer and the crisis blew over.

As 1873 drew to a close, the colonel sat brooding in his office at Fort Richardson. He had accomplished a great deal, but still had a long way to go. He could never be satisfied until the Quahadi were disarmed and forced onto the reservation.

Little did he know that this would happen in less than two years. His Fourth Cavalry would play a key role in their defeat. But the main cause would be the destruction of the buffalo and the Plains Indian way of life.

CHAPTER FIVE

The War for the Buffalo

"The buffalo is our money. It is our only resource. . . . We love them just as the white man does his money. Just as it makes a white man's heart feel to have his money carried away, so it makes us feel to see others killing and stealing our buffaloes, which are our cattle given to us by the Great Father above to provide us meat to eat and means to get things to wear."

—Chief Kicking Bird of the Kiowa

The buffalo had been losing ground for many years before the Civil War. They were shy creatures, and avoided human contact. As the line of settlement advanced, they moved away from ranges they had grazed for ages. By the 1860s, they had vanished from the eastern fringes of the Great Plains and the prairie states. Nevertheless, they still roamed the High Plains in the tens of millions.

Whites had never shown much interest in the lumbering beasts. They were not moneymakers like cattle, whose flesh could be eaten and skin turned into leather. Whites had not acquired a taste for buffalo meat; and besides, there was no way to ship large quantities of meat to eastern cities before the building of the railroads. The best market was in buffalo robes and tongues, but it was small. The robes, used as blankets in buggies and sleds, cost between ten and twenty dollars in New York City, depending on the quality. In the 1850s, the northern Plains tribes traded about one hundred thousand robes each year. There was no demand for dried or "flint" hides, and tanned skins were too soft for most purposes, but buffalo tongues were served as delicacies in big-city restaurants.

Traders bought buffalo robes with goods rather than money, cheating the Indians at every turn. An ordinary robe went for a pound of low-quality brown sugar or coffee. The best robes, embroidered with porcupine quills and painted with colorful designs representing weeks of painstaking work, brought twelve cups of sugar or six cups of coffee. But even at such ridiculous prices, traders took advantage; measuring cups usually had false bottoms and the sugar was mixed with sand. Alcohol, however, brought the highest profits. A gallon of pure alcohol was mixed with four gallons of water, a quart of black molasses, and a bottle of ginger "for taste." The result was a devil's brew that made braves see, not their guardian spirits, but demons. Drunken Indians killed one another, and even their own wives and children. Once addicted to this poison, they often exterminated the buffalo for miles around to obtain the hides to satisfy their liquor craving.

The Great Plains also attracted gun-toting tourists. Wealthy foreigners with time on their hands and money to burn killed not for food, like the Indian, but for thrills. Some, indeed, had no goal in life other than slaughtering big game in every corner of the globe. They shot wild boar in Europe, lions in Africa, and tigers in India. During the 1850s, they discovered the buffalo. The naturalist William T. Hornaday, who saw them in action, scorned them as pretend heroes. "There is," he wrote in disgust, "no kind of warfare against game animals too unfair, too disreputable, or too mean for white men to engage in if they can only do it with safety to their precious carcasses."[1]

The best known was an Irish nobleman, Sir George Gore. Where his pleasure was concerned, money was no object. Beginning in 1854, Gore spent a half million dollars (equal to ten million dollars in today's money) on a spectacular hunt lasting three years. Gore liked his comforts, even in the wilds of America. He brought forty servants, three cows for fresh milk, 112 thoroughbred horses, fifty hunting dogs, and scores of mules and oxen to pull his wagons. Not one to "rough it," he slept on a brass bed set up in a large tent with carpets to keep his lordly feet from touching the earth. When not out killing, he read leather-bound books from his traveling library and drank imported wines and champagne. But killing was his joy. By the time Gore returned to Ireland, he had shot 2,500 buffalo, 1,600 deer and elk, 105 bears, and smaller game too numerous to count.[2]

Killer-tourists destroyed buffalo in the thousands; railroads destroyed them by the hundreds of thousands. Called "shaggies" and "stinkers" by railroaders, they were so abundant that trains of the Atchison, Topeka & Santa Fe Railroad, building west of Dodge City, Kansas, often met herds ten miles long by four miles wide. The herds let nothing stand in their way, even moving trains. Ignoring the trains, animals on one side of a track would try to cross to the other no matter what stood in the way. "Each individual buffalo went at it with the desperation of despair," an engineer wrote, "plunging against or between locomotive and cars, just as the blind madness chanced to take them."[3] After having a few trains derailed, engineers stopped to allow the herds to cross. Though waiting often took hours, it was better than having to set a string of cars back on track.

Construction crews built up big appetites. Rather than haul beef to them by train, employers hired professional hunters to supply buffalo meat. William F. Cody, a Civil War veteran down on his luck in Nebraska, first made his name as a buffalo hunter. One day, he took a spill and a wounded bull chased him afoot. A group of soldiers nearby cheered and called him Buffalo Bill as he ran for his life.[4] They meant it as a joke, but that name made his fortune. Cody, who knew how to tell a tall story, told a newspaper reporter that he had turned on the charging beast, killing it with his knife. The story made him a celebrity back East. Seeing a good thing, he left hunting for show business. Buffalo Bill was the first Western showman-hero. Dime novels told of his exploits as a lawman, Indian fighter, and rescuer of women in distress—all pure fiction. He formed a circus, Buffalo Bill's Wild West, and became a millionaire.

The coming of the railroad offered great "sport" for travelers. Sometimes the animals' tongues, a delicacy, were cut out; usually, the bodies were left to rot where they fell.

Railroads brought hunting within reach of ordinary citizens. Inexpensive excursions left weekly from St. Louis, Missouri, bound for the buffalo country. When a herd was sighted, grazing peacefully, these "sportsmen" fired repeating rifles from the train windows. Trains occasionally stopped to allow passengers to cut out a few choice morsels—the tongue and hump ribs. These parts, weighing some fifty pounds, were all the meat taken from an animal of between one and two thousand pounds. Usually, however, the trains just plowed ahead, spewing death in every direction. Both sides of the tracks were lined for hundreds of miles with rotting carcasses and sun-bleached bones.

This was senseless butchery, but no threat to the buffalo's existence. Naturalists believed that Indians and whites killed five hundred thousand buffaloes a year between 1860 and 1870, or five million for the decade. Yet these losses seem to have had little effect on the buffalo as a whole. They were so numerous, it was said, that half a million could easily be killed each year without harming the herds. Perhaps. Unfortunately, an event on the other side of the world changed everything. In 1871, a German laboratory found a way to turn buffalo hides into leather for saddles, harness, luggage, jackets, and shoes. Better yet, buffalo leather made excellent drive belts for the machines that powered America's factories. Flint hides were now worth $3.50 apiece, more than most city workers earned in a day.

The slaughter began in Kansas. Dodge City, with its railroad yards and warehouses, was an ideal hunters' base. Hundreds of men left each week for the buffalo range or returned with wagonloads of hides to be sent east. Hunting teams operated smoothly and efficiently, like a piece of well-oiled machinery. A typical team consisted of one rifleman, the boss; five or six skinners; and two or three men to prepare the hides. The tools of the trade were simple: guns, ammunition, picks, shovels, axes, a grindstone, and dozens of butcher knives.

The rifleman had to be a good shot; in fact, a "sharpshooter," so called because of his Sharps rifle. Weighing sixteen pounds, the Sharps could drop the strongest buffalo at six hundred yards; equipped with a telescopic sight, it was deadly at three-quarters of a mile. Sharpshooters called it the "pizen slinger"; Indians said it "shoots today and kills tomorrow." A new rifle cost between eighty and one hundred dollars. Bullets cost twenty-five cents each, but could be reloaded and used again and again. Hunters' wagons always carried hundreds of pounds of lead to be molded into bullets, barrels of gunpowder, and firing caps.

There was little risk and no sportsmanship in hide hunting. Each morning, the boss started out on foot with two rifles. So long as he walked toward a herd in a straight line, it would not be alarmed; but if he stepped to the right or left, it would stampede. When he was about two hundred yards from the herd, the buffaloes on the outside began to grow restless. These were the sentries, old bulls or cows whose job it was to alert the others to danger.

Slowly sinking to the ground, the hunter hid behind some natural screen—a rock, a clump of grass, or a depression in the ground. He lay on his stomach, studying the herd to identify the leader. Then, placing a gun in a rest made from a forked stick, he took aim. His target was the leader's lungs, or "lights," not its heart. The buffalo was an unusually strong creature, and a bullet in the heart might not finish it off at once. "When you'd shoot a buffalo in the lights," a hunter recalled, "he'd throw blood out of his nose. Then he'd step backward a step or two, flop over, and

A hunter has made his "stand," and now the slaughtered animals await the skinner's knife.

die. If you shot him through the heart, he'd run four hundred yards before he'd fall, and he'd take the herd with him."[5]

The hunter tried to create a "stand," dropping each buffalo in such a way that the rest would not be scared away. George W. Reighard, an expert sharpshooter, explained: "Watching the herd carefully, I would note any movement on the part of any buffalo to take fright and start off. That would be my next victim. It would begin bleeding, lurching unsteadily, and would fall. Several would walk up and sniff at the two on the ground. They would throw up their heads and bawl, and one or two might start off. Then I must drop them. Sometimes a whole bunch would start. Then I must shoot quickly, dropping the leaders. That would turn the others back. The idea was to keep the buffaloes milling around in a restricted spot, shooting those on the outskirts that tried to move away." All the animals could see, Reighard continued, "was a little puff of white smoke now and then from a distant bush or rock. Usually that was not alarming. They generally would stay—milling, bawling, bewildered—until most of them were shot."[6]

After a while, the gun barrel overheated, expanding and causing the bullets to wobble. If the hunter continued to fire, the weapon might explode in his face. So he put it aside to cool and took up his spare. If this also became too hot, he cooled it with a bottle of water he carried for the purpose, or simply urinated on the barrel.

The two-gun system enabled hunters to rack up an enormous number of kills. Men like Zack Light and Tom Linton each shot between 2,300 and 3,000 buffaloes in a six-month period in Kansas; Joe McCombs downed 4,900 and Vic Smith 5,000. Tom Nixon once killed 204 buffaloes in a single stand, a record; another time, he dropped 120 in forty minutes. Wright Mooar, however, holds the lifetime record of 20,500 kills. Clearly, white hunters were better at killing buffaloes than Indians, who had been trained to hunt in childhood. But, for the Indian, killing was never a business. It was necessity and a way of life.[7]

The skinners took over from the sharpshooter. Skinners earned twenty-five cents per hide, so they must hustle to do well. Working in two-man teams, they rolled a buffalo onto its back and drove an iron spike through the skull to keep it in place. With butcher knives they slit its underside from tail to belly to chin and peeled off the hide. Or they tied a corner of the hide to a horse and cracked a whip. The horse lurched forward, tearing the hide off in one piece. Each hide was then stretched and pegged to the ground, hair side down, until dry. A fast team could skin a hundred buffaloes a day. Yet only one out of every three hides reached market, the rest having been ruined by improper handling or insect pests.

Buffalo hunting was not for the weak or the squeamish. Hunters were often outcasts from society who even the army would not accept. Many refused to give their names, preferring to be known only by nicknames. There was Shoot-'em-up Mike, Light-fingered Jack, Shotgun Collins, Prairie Dog Jake, and Dirtyface Jones. Shaggy and bearded, their clothes stiff with dried blood, sweat, and filth, they stank to high heaven and swarmed with "bed rabbits" (fleas). A traveler described the typical hunter: "He had long hair and was the dirtiest, greasiest, and smokiest mortal I had ever seen. He sat on a fleet horse, holding carelessly in his hands a .44 Sharps." Another noted that hunters were hard as nails. Unless a hunter was "head, neck, or gut shot, he was too damn stubborn and ornery to die!"[8]

Kansas became a slaughter pen. When the buffalo grew wary, hunters stationed themselves at the water holes and along streams. "Every drink of water, every mouthful of grass," wrote an eyewitness, "is at the expense of life, and the miserable animals, continually harassed, are driven into localities far from their natural haunts—anywhere to avoid the unceasing pursuit."[9] It did not help. The hunters followed, wiping out entire herds. It was said that a person could step from carcass to carcass, for hundreds of square miles, without touching the ground.

Dodge City prospered. Sheds at the railroad station, each

two hundred feet long by fifty feet wide, were packed ten feet high with buffalo hides. In the years 1872–1874, over 1.5 million hides left from this town alone, plus 7 million pounds of buffalo tongues.[10] Hunters had plenty of money, which attracted saloon keepers, cardsharps, dance hall girls, and gunmen. Dodge City became a drink-'em-up, shoot-'em-up hell-town. Nicknamed "Hell on the Plains," it was supposed to be the wickedest town in America.

Reports of the slaughter shocked people across the land. Protesters said that buffaloes, like people, were God's creatures and entitled to protection. Killing them for their skins alone was wicked and must be stopped, they insisted. High-ranking army officers agreed, claiming, as did one colonel, that the butchery "is as needless as it is cruel."[11] A number of western states and territories—Idaho, Wyoming, Montana, Colorado, Kansas—passed conservation laws. But these laws were ignored and the slaughter continued. One reason was greed: buffalo hides brought hard cash

Part of a pile of buffalo hides awaiting shipment at the Dodge City, Kansas, railway depot.

into a state. The main reason, however, was the U.S. Army.

Army leaders opposed conservation and encouraged the slaughter. Militarily, this made perfect sense. Their job was to fight Indians, not protect millions of animals. Exterminating the buffalo was the ultimate weapon in total war. With their food supply gone, the Plains tribes must surrender or starve. This is why General Sherman wanted to invite the world's sportsmen to "make one grand sweep" of the buffalo.[12] General Sheridan said it was a sentimental mistake to halt the killing. Calling hide hunters patriots, he said they should be given a medal for their efforts. "These men," he told state representatives, "are destroying the Indians' commissary; and it is a well-known fact that an army losing its base of supplies is placed at a great disadvantage. Send them powder and lead, if you will; but, for the sake of a lasting peace, let them kill, skin, and sell until the buffaloes are exterminated."[13] President Grant agreed. When Congress passed a conservation law, he vetoed it.

By the end of 1873, the buffalo were gone from Kansas. All that remained on the ranges north and west of Dodge City were a few strays and millions of putrid carcasses. There were so many carcasses that farmers drove herds of hogs to fatten on them. The High Plains of Texas, however, still teemed with buffalo. It was illegal for white hunters to cross into Texas according to the Treaty of Medicine Lodge. But, when hunters asked the advice of Major Richard Irving Dodge, the commander of Fort Dodge, he gave them his blessing. "Boys," he said, "if I were a buffalo hunter, I would hunt where the buffaloes are."[14] That blessing triggered the last Indian war on the southern Plains. The War for the Buffalo.

✕   ✕   ✕

The Kiowa tell how, in the long-ago time, before the oldest grandfather, the Great Spirit planted the Great Way Tree. The tree's boughs reached up to heaven, forming a pathway for all his creatures to come down to Earth. Lastly, a Kiowa man and woman came down to explore the creation. They walked about the High Plains of Texas, amazed at the vast emptiness. Weary from their wanderings, they returned to the Great Way Tree, and there they met the buffalo. "Here are the buffalo," the Great Spirit told his children. "They shall be your food and raiment, but in the day you shall see them perish from the face of the Earth, then know that the end of the Kiowa is near—and the Sun set."[15] And so it was.

In the spring of 1874, hide hunters crossed the Red River into Texas. They crossed knowing they were breaking the law and that the army would be looking the other way. But the Indians saw clearly. Quanah Parker often joined other Comanche and Kiowa war chiefs in fighting the hunters. Though Quanah did not torture captives, the others did. Dreading this, each hunter carried his "bite," a Sharps cartridge emptied of its gunpowder and filled with cyanide, a powerful poison. If capture seemed certain, he would "bite the bite," dying instantly. Indians never mutilated the bodies of suicides.

For every buffalo hunter killed, there was always another to take his place. Hunting was so profitable that whites gladly risked their lives. They were like a plague, an infection beyond the con-

Plains tribes were none too gentle with whites who invaded their hunting grounds. This drawing from Colonel George Armstrong Custer's book, *My Life on the Plains*, shows what happened to a group of professional buffalo hunters taken by surprise in their camp.

Together with Quanah Parker, the Kiowa chief Lone Wolf led his men into action against the buffalo hunters at Adobe Walls.

trol of any war chief or tribe. Only the Great Spirit, it seemed, could save the buffalo.

One man knew how. He was Esa-tai, whose name means "Rear-End-of-a-Wolf" or "Little Wolf," a young Quahadi medicine man and a prophet. Men like Esa-tai were not unusual among the Native Americans. When things became desperate, prophets had always arisen. During the 1750s, for example, the Delaware Prophet rallied the forest tribes by telling of a dream-journey in which the Great Spirit promised to help them drive the English into the sea. The result was an uprising that claimed hundreds of lives, Indians and whites, before being crushed.

Esa-tai claimed to have special medicine. Bullets could not harm him, he insisted, without a hint of doubt in his voice. He had performed miracles such as bringing the dead back to life and vomiting a wagonload of cartridges, which he swallowed once again. The Quahadi had heard such stories before, and were not impressed. But when Esa-tai predicted that a comet would blaze across the sky for five days, and it did, they began to change their minds. And when he said a severe drought would come, and it did, they believed he could do anything. His fame spread to other Comanche bands, then among other tribes, just as the hide hunters were swarming into Texas. In desperation, they begged him to speak the thoughts of the Great Spirit.

Esa-tai called a council late in June of 1874. The council met near the boundary of the reservation, where Elk Creek joins the North Fork of the Red River. It was a solemn occasion, a religious occasion. Never before had the Comanche come together at one time and in one place. Never before had so many tribes—Kiowa, Arapaho, Southern Cheyenne—joined them in a common effort. But the stakes were higher than ever before. If the Great Spirit would not help them, and soon, they were doomed.

Warriors gathered around the council fire, their weapons in their hands, their faces streaked with black paint. The fire hissed and roared, spitting sparks into the night sky. Since the Quahadi hosted the council, Quanah Parker, their paramount war chief, presided. One by one, he called on the visiting chiefs to speak. Stone Calf spoke for the Southern Cheyenne. Lone Wolf and White Horse spoke for the Kiowa. They told of the whites' broken promises, of hunger and despair on the reservations, of buffalo graveyards stretching to the horizon and beyond. Quanah himself spoke bitterly of Bad Hand Mackenzie's pursuit across the Staked Plain.

Finally, Esa-tai stepped into the circle of light. His face was hairless and unlined by wrinkles. He was naked except for a breechclout, moccasins, and a red cloth wound around his waist. For decoration, he had a red-tipped hawk feather in his hair, wide silver bracelets on his forearms, and earrings of rattlesnake rattles. Around his neck he wore a tiny medicine bag made from the skin of *Esa*, the wolf, his guardian spirit.

A small drum began to beat as Esa-tai leaned over the fire. Slowly he washed his hands, face, and chest in the purifying smoke. "Great Spirit, make us strong," he chanted softly. "Esa, our brother, show us what to do." The smoke swirled around him, carrying his words upward to the heavens. Fire, smoke, sparks, and drum mingled with his chant to create a magical spell. To the assembled warriors, Esa-tai and the Great Spirit had become one.

Suddenly, the drumming stopped. Esa-tai spread his arms and spoke in a ringing voice. He told of many things, of how he had visited the Great Spirit and what he had learned in the world beyond the clouds. "O chiefs and brothers," he said, "behold me, Esa-tai, son of the wolf. My medicine is strong. My spirit left my body and went far away, up the path of the Milky Way and the stars. I came to the place of the Great Spirit; the Great Father of the Indians, who is greater than and higher than the white man's God. I was weary with the far journey. My feet could scarcely move and my tongue was dry with thirst and my belly thin with hunger. My moccasins were strings and my robe could not keep

Esa-tai was a Comanche medicine man who called for the extermination of the buffalo hunters, claiming the Great Spirit had taught him how to make the Indians bulletproof.

out the terrible cold. But the Great Father said: 'Ho, here is a brave man and a strong warrior who could make this journey.' A woman gave me food and drink. I was warm and happy."[16]

The Great Spirit opened his heart to the wolf prophet. "I will take pity on the people," he promised. "I will make them strong in war and they shall drive the white men away. The . . . tribes that dig in the ground and have made peace with the white men, they shall very soon pass away. There shall not be any of them left. Those Comanches and Kiowas and others who stay on the reservation shall pass away just like them. Only the warriors shall be strong and increase. They shall hold all the land, going where they please. The buffalo shall come back everywhere, so that there shall be feasting and plenty in the lodges."[17]

The Great Spirit told Esa-tai to give his message to any who would listen. He also told him how to mix medicine paint that would make its wearers bulletproof. As Esa-tai spoke, he fixed his eyes on Quanah, a devoted follower. "That is so," said Quanah, who believed his every word.[18]

Esa-tai threw back his head and howled like a wolf. Then he picked up a handful of cedar bark and signaled the drummer. Once again the smoke swirled around the prophet. Once again the drum throbbed, louder and louder, then stopped abruptly. Once again Esa-tai began to chant:

O Great Father, have pity.
O Great Father, make us strong.
Make our arrows swift,
Make our bows powerful.
Give us sharp lances.
Great Father, have pity.[19]

The low chant became a loud war whoop. Esa-tai began to dance with outstretched arms, moving them up and down with the grace of a high-flying eagle. Suddenly there was an arrow in his hand. It must have come from the Great Spirit, warriors thought, since no one had seen it before. Esa-tai waved it over his head, and in an instant a second arrow appeared in his other hand, and then a third. "These are medicine arrows sent by the Great Spirit," he said, holding them out. "My brothers, the Great Father will give you power. You shall drive out the white men and the Great Father will bring the buffalo back again. He has told me so when I was taken up to see him." Then Esa-tai gave one last wolf howl and sat down.[20]

The warriors' very blood caught fire. Esa-tai had spoken! The Great Spirit had spoken through him! They had strong medicine. Victory was assured. They would destroy the hide hunters and drive the whites from the Plains. The buffalo would return and the tribes would live in the old way forever. Still, a few held back. When some of the older chiefs warned against Esa-tai's wild visions, they were called "toothless squaws." The War for the Buffalo would be a young man's war.

The next two days were filled with excitement. Braves danced and sang, fought mock battles and captured mock forts. On the second evening, they left camp. No one knows their exact number; participants put it between seven and twelve hundred. But even at the lower figure, it was the largest war party ever seen on the southern Plains. Quanah Parker led the Comanche, by far the largest group.

Their target was Adobe Walls on the bank of the Canadian River, 150 miles south of Dodge City. "The Walls," as whites called it, was actually the ruins of a trading post abandoned thirty years earlier. Early in 1874, they were taken over by Dodge City merchants as a hunters' supply base. The settlement consisted of a saloon, two stores, and a blacksmith shop built around a horse corral.

On the night of June 26, twenty-eight men and one woman were at The Walls. The men were all hunters, or former hunters, armed with Sharps rifles. Among them was Bat Masterson, soon to win fame as a lawman, and Billy Dixon, one of the best sharpshooters in the West. His story, as told to his wife, Olive, later

Known to his friends as "Bat," William Barclay Masterson was one of the most famous lawmen in the Old West. He began his career as a buffalo hunter and was among the defenders of Adobe Walls.

became a popular book: *Life of "Billy" Dixon: Plainsman, Scout and Pioneer*. It is the best eyewitness account of the events at Adobe Walls.

It was a warm night, and most of the men slept on the ground, near the buildings. Indians were always a danger, they knew, and they had their bites ready—just in case. But since there had not been any attacks in the vicinity, they took no precautions. They should have.

Several miles to the west, other men were preparing for battle. Years later, Quanah recalled that "we make medicine, paint faces," and checked weapons.[21] As each man finished, he either went to sleep or sat up smoking tobacco and talking to friends in low whispers. Esa-tai spent the night alone in a clump of trees along the Canadian River. There he sat, totally naked, having painted himself and his horse a brilliant yellow. Come morning, he would not fight, but stay on a ridge overlooking The Walls and pray to the Great Spirit. His medicine, no less than the braves' courage, would bring victory.

Adobe Walls slept. But at 2 A.M., June 27, there was loud *crack*, like a gunshot. "Clear out!" someone shouted. A support beam had broken, threatening to bring down the roof of the saloon. The men nearest the building awoke with a start and began to shore up the damaged beam. By the time they finished two hours later, the sky was brightening in the east. Some returned to their bedrolls for a little more shut-eye, others took the free drinks offered by the grateful saloonkeeper. Not Billy Dixon. Since he was already up, he decided to get an early start.

So had Quanah, who was riding at the head of his braves. They moved quietly, but some overeager youths began to pull ahead of the main body. Quanah passed the word: "You go too fast. No good to go too fast."[22] Yet they were so eager for action that the chiefs let them go ahead. Digging their heels into their horses' sides, the whole war party sprang forward. But in the half-darkness, more than one horse got its leg caught in a prairie dog hole. And more than one horse and rider went down, tumbling over and over. The others swept past them at a full gallop.

At that very moment, Dixon's horse raised its head and pricked its ears. Looking up, Billy saw a dark V-shape coming from the west. Gaining speed, it spread out like the arms of a fan. Indians! Hundreds of Indians were whipping their horses and heading straight for The Walls! "There was never a more splendidly barbaric sight," Dixon recalled.

> Hundreds of warriors, the flower of the fighting men of the southwestern Plains tribes, mounted upon their finest horses, armed with guns and lances, and carrying heavy shields of thick buffalo hide, were coming like the wind. Over all was splashed the rich colors of red, vermillion and ocher, on the bodies of the men, on the bodies of the running horses. Scalps dangled from bridles, gorgeous war-bonnets fluttered their plumes, bright feathers dangled from the tails and manes of the horses, and the bronzed, half-naked bodies of the riders glittered with ornaments of silver and brass. Behind this head-long charging host stretched the Plains, on whose horizon the rising sun was lifting its morning fires. The warriors seemed to emerge from this glowing background. . . . War-whooping had a very appreciable effect upon the roots of one's hair.[23]

In other words, the hair stood up on the back of his neck.

Dixon fired a single shot and made a dash for the saloon. Alerted by his shot, the hunters were already barricading themselves in the buildings. But the Sadler brothers, Ike and Shorty, were sound asleep in their wagon outside the saloon and had not heard Dixon's warning. They were killed and scalped. So was their dog, a big Labrador that always slept at their feet. He had defended his masters so fiercely that a brave "scalped" him by cutting a strip of fur from his side.

The raiders were off to a good start, but not good enough. The opening minutes of this attack show the basic difference between white soldiers and Indian braves. Enjoying a twenty-five-to-one advantage, soldiers would have smashed in the doors at the outset. That might have cost dozens of lives, but they would have gained their objective quickly. Braves, however, always tried to avoid guaranteed losses. As they closed in around the buildings, they used their favorite riding trick. They circled at full speed, dropping over the sides of their horses by sliding one arm through a loop braided into the animals' manes and with one leg flung over their backs. Safe behind these moving shields, they shot arrows and bullets from under the horses' necks. Yet they would not press the attack.

Even so, it was pretty hot inside the buildings. "The bullets poured in like hail," Dixon recalled.[24] Lead slugs buried themselves in the walls and furniture. Windowpanes shattered, sending glass splinters whizzing through the air. The hunters, barefoot and in their underwear, banged away with their Sharps rifles.

Mrs. William Olds, the wife of a storekeeper, was a small, frail-looking woman in her late twenties. When the shooting began, she stood by a window with a rifle. Her hands trembled, but she kept pulling the trigger. And each time she did, the rifle's kickback spun her half around. If defeat became certain, the hunters vowed that "none would have suffered themselves to be taken alive or have permitted Mrs. Olds to be captured."[25] That, fortunately, was unnecessary. Only one man, a hunter named Billy Tyler, was killed by the enemy during the siege. Mrs. Olds's husband accidentally shot himself in the head, dying instantly.

Quanah, meantime, ordered repeated charges, which he led in person. Once he whirled his horse around, backing it into a door in an effort to smash it down. But the door held. During another assault, a Comanche named Ho-we-a fell wounded in front of the saloon door. Riding through a hail of bullets, the chief leaned over, swept Ho-we-a off the ground with one arm, and carried him out of danger. Moments later, Quanah himself felt the sting of a bullet.

He had just brought Ho-we-a to safety when his horse collapsed with a bullet in the heart. Pitched to the ground, Quanah rolled behind a rotting buffalo carcass. The carcass stank terribly, but he pressed himself into it as bullets kicked up dust on either side. Suddenly, he felt a terrific stinging sensation between his neck and shoulder. A bullet had struck him from *behind*, grazing his skin and drawing a little blood. He was all right, except that his right arm was paralyzed for the rest of the day. At first, he thought a brave had shot at him by mistake. But no braves were to be seen in the rear. That was even more terrifying than his close call. Quanah, like all Comanches, explained strange happenings in terms of magic, not science. The whites' medicine, clearly, allowed their bullets to whip around a man and hit him in the back! Quanah, of course, had been struck by a bullet that rebounded after glancing off a rock.

The hunters' buffalo guns outranged the Indians' rifles by hundreds of yards. Once the hunters got into the swing of things, they shot often and well. The sound of the heavy rifles echoed across the plain. Warriors found that hiding behind their moving shields was no protection. Like Quanah, their horses were shot from under them. Unlike him, however, their riders were picked off as they raced for cover. Gradually, the assaults became fewer, each being carried out with less enthusiasm than the one before. By afternoon, the braves withdrew to a ridge facing Adobe Walls. The guns fell silent.

At about four o'clock, the hunters came out for a look-see. Bodies littered the ground. All their animals—fifty-six horses and twenty-eight oxen—lay dead, feathered arrows sticking in their bodies. Thirteen dead Indians were counted around the buildings and as far out on the prairie as they dared to go. After taking some shields and war bonnets as souvenirs, they buried the Sadlers and Billy Tyler in the same grave. The animal carcasses, already decaying, were dragged away from the buildings. The Indian bodies were decapitated and the heads nailed to the corral posts. One reason for doing this was pure orneriness; the hunters were angry and took it out on the corpses. The other was a warning: either the attacks stopped, or more braves would spend eternity minus their heads.

The Indians were discouraged. On the second day, June 28, they had a council on a patch of open ground behind a low hill, out of sight of Adobe Walls. Esa-tai had lied, a Cheyenne shouted, waving his riding whip in the medicine man's face. He had promised to make them bulletproof and to give them an easy victory. What nonsense! "If the white man's bullets cannot hurt you," another cried, "go down and bring back my son's body!"[26]

Esa-tai blamed the Cheyenne. Before the attack, some Cheyennes had killed and eaten a skunk, a delicacy among the southern Plains tribes. Unfortunately, the skunk was also one of Esa-tai's guardian spirits, and killing it destroyed his medicine, he said. That made sense to the warriors. But as they spoke, Esa-tai's horse, gleaming in its magic paint, shuddered and fell dead, blood spurting from a bullet hole in its forehead. How could the whites hit a target they could not see, and at such a distance? As with Quanah the day before, there could be only one answer. "The white men have a very strong medicine," Esa-tai explained. "Shoot today, maybeso kill you tomorrow."[27] (The whites' "medicine" was a stray shot that landed in the right place at the right time.) From then on the braves made no more charges, but kept their distance. Without horses, they knew, no one was leaving Adobe Walls.

That afternoon, however, a hunter named George Bellfield arrived with his outfit. Bellfield had no idea that Adobe Walls was besieged, and for some reason Quanah let him pass. No sooner did he arrive, when it was decided to send to Dodge City for help. Henry Lease, another hunter, volunteered for the dangerous trip. Borrowing one of Bellfield's horses, he set out after sundown. At the same time, two other men went to alert any hunters who might be in the vicinity.

On the third day, the chiefs held a council on top of a bluff east of Adobe Walls. The hunters saw them as black dots outlined against the eastern sky. Tiny as they were, they were still large enough for Billy Dixon. Taking aim, he fired a single shot from his Sharps rifle. Moments later, Quanah's friend To-hah-kah fell from his horse. The others galloped to a clump of trees. After a few minutes, two braves ran out on foot to drag the body away. Dixon's famous "long shot" was later measured at 1,538 yards, nearly seven-eighths of a mile, an all-time record with the Sharps rifle.

Dixon's shot ended the siege. Convinced that the whites' medicine was stronger than theirs, the war party melted away. Left behind were at least 15 dead; some participants put the number at between 70 and 115. The true figure will never be known. But whatever it was, the Indians had suffered a defeat. Meantime, as news of the siege spread, hunters made a beeline for the trading post. By the sixth day, about 100 men had arrived. A 40-man rescue party came from Dodge City the following week. Henry Lease had come through without a scratch.

Adobe Walls was soon abandoned. Fearing for their lives, most hunters returned to Kansas. They'd had enough of Indians and were not shy about saying so. Most went into other lines of work, even bought train tickets for their homes in the East. Billy Dixon became an army scout. Bat Masterson began a career as a lawman. The storekeepers lost everything. After they left, the Comanche burned their buildings to the ground. There would be no hide hunting in Texas that summer.

The siege of Adobe Walls was the beginning, not the end, of the War for the Buffalo. "Pretty soon," Quanah said years later, "I take all young men, go warpath to Texas."[28] He was not alone. Determined to defend their way of life, war parties spread terror across Texas, New Mexico, Colorado, Kansas, and the Indian Territory. Ranches were raided and cattle driven off. Stagecoaches and wagon trains were attacked. Hide hunters, those foolish enough to stay out on the Plains, were butchered. A total of 190 whites were killed within two months.

During the Battle of Adobe Walls, Billy Dixon set an all-time record for distance and accuracy with his Sharps hunting rifle.

Horse soldiers were nowhere to be seen. They seemed to be clinging to their forts, like newborn buffalo calves to their mothers. That was strange behavior for men who had been so aggressive in the past. Perhaps Adobe Walls had been an Indian victory after all. Perhaps the army was too scared to go after them.

✕　✕　✕

General Sherman had no more patience for Indians. Early in July, he drew up a plan of action. It was a harsh plan, worthy of a believer in total war, and President Grant approved it without hesitation. There would be no more peace commissions, no more speeches, no more treaties with Indians. Never again would Indians be permitted off their reservations. All "friendlies" were to report to their reservation headquarters to be enrolled by name. Those who failed to enroll, or who missed the daily roll calls, would be treated as "hostiles." And may God help them, for the army would not! They would be attacked on sight and the survivors treated as prisoners of war. Their chiefs would be tried in military courts and given long jail terms or executed.

General Sheridan prepared the actual battle plan. It called for the biggest campaign ever waged against the southern Plains tribes. During July and August, troops poured into the frontier forts. When ready, columns of cavalry were to stab into the Staked Plain from five directions. Colonel Nelson A. Miles was to head south with the Sixth Cavalry from Fort Dodge, Kansas; Major William R. Price's Eighth Cavalry east from Fort Bascom, New Mexico; and Colonel John W. Davidson's black Tenth Cavalry west from Fort Sill, Indian Territory, supported by Colonel George P. Buell's Eleventh Cavalry from Fort Richardson, Texas. Last but not least, Colonel Ranald S. Mackenzie's Fourth Cavalry would strike north from Fort Concho, Texas, on the Colorado River. The columns were to move back and forth, scouring the area, their trails crisscrossing again and again, until they found the hostiles. Their orders were brutally simple: "Drive all the Indians onto the reservation or kill them."[29]

Colonel Miles made contact first. His column had marched for weeks in 110-degree heat, the summer of 1874 being one of the hottest in memory. On August 30, Miles found a large band of Southern Cheyenne near Tule Canyon on the eastern edge of the Staked Plain. He pressed the attack with cavalry charges supported by Gatling guns, an early type of machine gun. Though the braves retreated, Miles lacked the supplies to finish the job. As he withdrew, a norther swept in, bringing torrential rains. Moments earlier, troopers had been sweating and eating dust; now they shivered and plodded through deep mud. The Cheyenne were so wet that their hands became wrinkled, hence their name for the action: "The Wrinkled-Hand Chase."

Colonel Mackenzie combed the same area four weeks later. It was like chasing shadows. His scouts found lots of Indian signs, but no Indians. One day, they saw buffalo running west of Tule Canyon as if they were being chased. Expecting an attack, Bad Hand made sure his horses were securely tied when he camped in the canyon that night. Sure enough, at ten o'clock Quahadi warriors tried to stampede the horses, only to be driven off by alert guards. Apart from this skirmish, Indians were nowhere to be seen. It was fall, the time when they prepared for winter. Somewhere, out there on the Staked Plain, the bands were gathering. But where?

The answer came on September 27. A Fourth Cavalry patrol met some Comancheros near where the buffalo had been running. Their boss was Jose Piedad Tafoya, an old-timer who knew the Staked Plain like his backyard. Bad Hand asked about Quanah Parker, politely. "*No se,*" he replied, "I don't understand." The colonel hung Tafoya from a propped-up wagon tongue until he did understand. Yes, he knew the Quahadi chief. Yes, he knew where the Indians had gathered. And, yes, he would draw a map. Years later, when Quanah learned of Tafoya's betrayal, he promised to broil the old Comanchero alive if he ever caught him. Luckily for Tafoya, he never did.[30]

The Indians were in Palo Duro Canyon on the Prairie Dog Town Fork of the Red River. The Palo Duro, an Indian term meaning "hard wood," is known today as the Grand Canyon of Texas. It is grand, and stunningly beautiful. During millions of years, the river had cut (and still cuts) deeply into the land, revealing bands of red, brown, white, and orange rock on either side. For centuries, the Palo Duro sheltered the Indians from the northers of the Plains. The cedar, cottonwood, and wild cherry that grew along the river provided fuel, lodge poles, and arrows. Though the canyon is six miles from rim to rim and eight hundred feet deep, the surrounding plain is so flat that it is invisible until you are right on the edge. And no American had ever stood there.

Mackenzie sent chief of scouts Lieutenant William Thompson, Sergeant John Charlton, and a Tonkawa named Job to locate the enemy camps. Arriving early in the afternoon, after a twenty-five-mile ride, they peered over the edge of the Palo Duro. Fantastic! Eight hundred feet below, they saw long rows of tipis and horse herds grazing peacefully on the lush grass. The scouts could hardly believe their good luck. Not only had they found the main Comanche winter camp, but also that of the Kiowa and Southern Cheyenne. "Take a good look, boys," said Charlton. "It won't be long before a sight like this will be gone forever from the Plains."[31]

The scouts reported to Mackenzie shortly after sundown. Leaving his supply wagons in Tule Canyon, he took the Fourth Cavalry on an all-night march. They reached the Palo Duro Canyon at dawn on September 28.

Bad Hand bellied up to the edge and peered over. In the half-light he saw a narrow path zigzagging down the steep canyon wall. Turning to his chief of scouts, he gave the order: "Mr. Thompson, take your men down and open the fight."[32]

The Tonkawas led the way, followed by the regiment. The path was too steep for mounted men, so they went on foot, single file, leading their horses. Even so, men and horses stumbled and slid, kicking up little landslides of pebbles every few feet. They had gone most of the way when a lookout, posted on a rock ledge, saw them. Instantly he gave a war whoop and waved a red blanket to warn of the approaching danger. The bullet that silenced him echoed down the canyon. A Kiowa warrior heard the shot and saw the first troopers scrambling onto the canyon floor. But instead of leaping onto his horse and spreading the alarm, he fired four shots before running into his tipi to put on war paint. The shots were heard in a nearby Kiowa village, and ignored. The Kiowa felt so safe that they could not imagine the cavalry could find them, much less reach them in their stronghold. The shots must have been fired by an early-morning deer hunter, they thought.

By the time they saw their danger, it was too late. The Fourth Cavalry formed ranks and charged. Few warriors bothered about war paint now. All that mattered was covering the escape of their women and children. As these leaped onto their horses and fled down the valley, braves scrambled up the canyon's northeast wall and opened fire on the advancing troopers.

Signs of panic were everywhere. "As we galloped along we passed village after village of Indian lodges both on the right and left, all empty and totally abandoned," Robert Carter, now a captain, recalled. "The ground was strewn with buffalo robes, blankets, and every imaginable thing, in fact, that the Indians had in the way of property—all of which had been hastily collected and a vain attempt made by the squaws to gather up and save, but finding the troopers up so rapidly they were forced to drop their goods . . . to save themselves from capture. Numbers of their pack animals were running around loose with their packs on, while others stood tied to trees—all having been abandoned by their owners, who were pressed so hard by our command that they had to hastily flee to the shelter of the rocks that towered above us to the right and left."[33]

The warriors slowed the cavalry long enough for their loved ones to clamber onto the Staked Plain. Indian losses were four killed and perhaps eight wounded; one trooper, a bugler, was shot in the stomach, but recovered. That recovery was a minor miracle in itself; gut-shot men rarely survived.

Measured in terms of Civil War battles, the Battle of Palo Duro Canyon was hardly a skirmish. Numbers, however, do not tell the whole story. Though few Indians were killed, and none taken prisoner, they had suffered a shattering defeat.

Mackenzie knew that the tools of war are as important as the warriors who use them. In saving themselves, the Indians had abandoned most of their winter supplies, plus hundreds of good rifles. All were burned. Better yet, 1,424 horses were rounded up during the cavalry's dash along the canyon floor. Next day, they were driven to the edge of Tule Canyon and shot by firing squads. Bad Hand remembered the lesson Quanah taught him in 1872 and would never again give Indians the chance to retake their horses. Mounds of bones lay there for many years, until a Texan hauled them away for fertilizer. Legend has it that, on the nights of the Comanche moon, a phantom herd of riderless horses can still be seen galloping along the canyon's rim.[34]

The slaughter of the horses ended the first stage of Mackenzie's campaign. During the following months, he searched north and west of the Palo Duro. Fourth Cavalry patrols explored every canyon, visited every water hole, in an area of hundreds of square miles. He fought two dozen small actions— so small he never reported them. Yet he was less interested in killing Indians than in keeping them off balance. After all, a "horse Indian" minus his horse was a sad person indeed. Always on the run, scarcely able to keep ahead of the cavalry, he had little chance to hunt for the winter.

Winter came early that year. Northers lashed the Staked Plain, bringing snow and subzero temperatures. By late December, even the dogged Mackenzie had to give up the chase. The Fourth Cavalry moved into winter quarters at Fort Richardson. No matter. Sooner or later, he knew, Mother Nature would bring the hostiles to their senses.

The War for the Buffalo was over.

On the White Man's Road

"With keen foresight [Quanah] recognized the inevitable, that the Indian had to give way before the superior force of the white man, so he set about to make the best of the new conditions and persuade his people to do likewise."

— A. C. Greene, *The Last Captive*

"The Indians survived our best intention of wiping them out, and since the tide turned they have weathered our good intentions toward them, which can be much more deadly."

—John Steinbeck, *America and Americans*

 It was as if the Great Spirit had forsaken The People. The golden times, the years of freedom and prosperity, lay behind them. Their world had turned topsy-turvy. Once again they were a people afoot, a poor people who had lost most of their possessions. Even if they still had some horses, these were of little use. Weakened by exposure and overwork, they had become pitiful bags of bones. So had their masters. Hunger stalked the High Plains as it had not done for 150 years. Babies froze, and older children cried for food and warmth. Once in a while braves killed a buffalo, but mostly there were only nuts, grubs, and field mice to eat.

One by one, the bands decided they could not survive the winter. So, one by one, they made the long journey to Fort Sill. Lone Wolf brought in his Kiowas first, in February 1875. The Southern Cheyenne arrived a few weeks later, followed by nearly all the Comanche bands. They were a pathetic sight. "A more wretched and poverty-stricken community than these it would be difficult to imagine," an official said of the

Southern Cheyenne. "Bereft of lodges, and the most ordinary cooking apparatus; with no ponies, or other means of transportation for wood or water; half starved, [wearing] scarcely anything that could be called clothing, they were truly objects of pity."[1]

There were no welcoming committees at Fort Sill. The moment they arrived, their horse gear and weapons were seized and burned. Their remaining horses were either sold to whites or shot on the prairie west of the fort. The women and children were placed in detention camps guarded by soldiers. War chiefs were handcuffed and put in cells in the basement of the guard house; seventy-four were later sent to the military prison at Fort Marion in St. Augustine, Florida. Braves were confined in an unfinished icehouse, the shell of a building with walls, a stone floor, but no roof. There they lived in canvas pup tents set up against the walls with a row of campfires down the middle for warmth. Once a day, a supply wagon pulled up and soldiers flung chunks of red meat over the walls as if they were feeding zoo animals. "They fed us like we were lions," a brave recalled.[2]

Only the Quahadi were still at large. Somehow they survived the brutal winter, but by spring they also admitted defeat. Late in April, J. J. Sturm, the post interpreter, left Fort Sill with three Comanches he knew and trusted. These men also knew Quanah Parker, and had a pretty good idea where he might be found. Nine days later, they reached the Quahadi camp near Tule Canyon. Sturm carried a message from Bad Hand Mackenzie. The colonel gave them an offer they could not—*dared* not—refuse. If they surrendered without a fuss, he promised on his word of honor, they would not be harmed. But if they refused, he would not rest until he exterminated them. The choice was theirs.

Quanah needed to be alone. Leaving camp, he went to the top of a low, sandy hill. Drawing a buffalo robe over his head, he wrestled with his conscience. As a war chief, he preferred fighting to the bitter end. He hated the reservation and all it stood for. He had only contempt for Indians who left the warpath to dig in the soil. But could he lead women and children to their doom? All the other chiefs, men he respected, had been unable to do so. They surrendered. Still, could he be right and they wrong? The more he questioned himself, the more questions he had. Hard questions. Questions without answers. If only the Great Spirit would give him a sign!

Peering out from his blanket, he saw movement in the sky above and on the earth below. Below was a wolf. *Esa* turned his head toward Quanah's hilltop and howled, then ran off to the east. Eastward, toward Fort Sill! At that very moment, the shadow of an eagle sped along the ground in the same direction. The Great Spirit had spoken, and Quanah obeyed. He would take his people to the reservation.[3]

The Quahadi took nearly a month to reach the fort. In his diary, Sturm described a calm, even a happy, journey. The men hunted as best they could with the horses they still had, while the women made lodge covers and dried buffalo meat. One day they found an abandoned wagon, which they drove as fast as it would go, loaded with every child who could hang on. On June 2, they surrendered to Bad Hand Mackenzie. Coming almost eight years after the Treaty of Medicine Lodge, their surrender marked the end of warfare on the southern Plains. Only fifty Comanche holdouts remained outside the reservation, but not for long.

Quanah's surrender brought about a change in the hard-bitten Mackenzie. Bad Hand was a ruthless fighter, but also a decent man. As a professional soldier, he admired courage, even in enemies. And none had fought more courageously and honorably than Quanah. True, he had killed whites, but in defense of his own country. He had never promised the whites anything other than a fight if they invaded the Staked Plain, and therefore had broken no treaty. Such a man, and such a band, deserved special treatment. Upon learning that the Quahadi were coming in, the colonel wrote General Sheridan, "I think better of this band than of any other on the reserve. . . . I shall let them down as easily as I can."[4]

**Chief Quanah Parker
about the year 1890**

Quanah convinced Mackenzie that he had made the right decision. As soon as he arrived at Fort Sill, he told the colonel about Cynthia Ann. He cherished the memory of his white mother, and "for that reason I will not do anything bad."[5] That was a solemn pledge.

Bad Hand took him at his word. Soon after his arrival, he sent Quanah to bring in the holdouts. If the chief met any cavalry, he was to hand the commanding officer his written orders, signed by the colonel himself. Any officer who gave trouble would have to explain why to him, Mackenzie, in person. Quanah returned with twenty-one braves he located on the Plains.

He also persuaded Herman Lehman to come in. Herman had been kidnapped by Apaches as a child and fled to the Comanche after killing a medicine man. Now seventeen, he dreaded white people. As Quanah rode with him toward Fort Sill, the youth wheeled his horse around and sped away as if he had seen the devil. Quanah followed, catching him after a four-mile chase. Seeing the boy's terror, he said he could stay with the Quahadi and not give himself up to the soldiers. Herman lived with Quanah's band for three years and was adopted into the chief's family. One day, Quanah told him that his mother was still alive and asked if he wanted to go to her. "I told him no; that the Indians were my people," Herman recalled. Finally, after some gentle persuasion, Herman returned to Texas. In time he settled down, married a white woman, and raised a family. But he always considered himself a man of The People.[6]

Meantime, the Comanche faced another challenge. By surrendering, they had to adjust to a new way of life or vanish as a group. For them, it was like entering a time machine in one age and exiting in another. Their grandfathers had made stone-tipped arrows and used a few metal tools obtained from Spanish traders. Their fathers had fought with iron knives and guns. They prized factory-made cloth hauled across the Plains by steam-belching "iron horses" galloping over ribbons of steel. Their captors spoke to each other over the "talking wire," telegraph lines that linked towns and forts. To survive, The People would have to cross centuries in a single lifetime, journeying from the Stone Age to the Modern Age.

They were fortunate in having Quanah Parker at this critical time. He had been a great warrior, but so had many others. What set him apart was not his war skills, but his peace skills. We do not know how these developed, since most of his life before the reservation was never written down. But once on the reservation, he quickly matured as a tribal leader. Quanah let bygones be bygones. He earned Bad Hand Mackenzie's trust. When he met Billy Dixon, and learned of his long shot at Adobe Walls, he shook his hand and became his good friend. Government agents found that having the chief on their side made their jobs easier.

A highly intelligent man, Quanah understood that confrontation must give way to cooperation. Or, to use the old adage, "to get along you must go along." Operating in both the Comanche and white worlds, he became what social scientists call a "culture broker," a middleman between two very different peoples, explaining each to the other. Quanah's genius lay in knowing when to give in and when to dig in his heels. Thus, he followed the white man's road for the good of his people, while skillfully protecting their heritage.

Quanah's skills were appreciated and rewarded by the authorities. Before long, they recognized him as the principal chief of the Comanches, something they had never had before. His ability to get along with whites made him unpopular with some. They called him a "half-breed," a "half-blood," and a "white man's Indian." The majority, however, knew better. They knew that, although he was of mixed race, he was Comanche in his heart and soul. A brave named Apache John said it best: "he is just like light, you strike a match in a dark room and there is light; that is the way with Quanah, wherever he is is light."[7]

Admiration, however, could not feed the hungry. Indian agents, officials who looked after reservation tribes, were allowed three dollars a month to feed each person. This did not buy very much food even in those days. But food was not expected to be a problem, because shortages could be made up by hunting; there were still plenty of buffalo in Texas. During the early years, however, Indians were not allowed off the reservation for any reason. It had taken a war to get them there, and the government was not about to let them go. Nor were the *Tejanos*. Texas Rangers shot any Comanche they found south of the Red River; in one incident, five were killed and their heads put on display in the town of Jacksboro.[8] It was even made illegal for Comanches to enter the state of Texas.

News that the Comanche were penned up on the reservation triggered the last, and greatest, buffalo hunts. Early in 1876, fifteen hundred hide hunters were operating on the Staked Plain. They went everywhere, and their rifles could be heard booming all over the countryside.

The slaughter was terrific. Fort Griffin, a rail depot east of Fort Worth, became another Dodge City. Night and day its streets rang with the shouts of hunters, wagon drivers, cowboys, and off-duty soldiers wearing "drinking jewelry," rings made of twisted horseshoe nails. From saloons and gambling halls came the sounds of drunken laughter, breaking furniture, and gunshots. When the wind shifted, it carried a putrid odor from the western Plains. "The country around Fort Griffin," a townsman wrote, "was covered with buffalo skeletons . . . till it was dangerous to ride out [at] a trot; and in town there was a stack of buffalo hides as long as a city block, as high as a man could reach, throwing hides out of a wagon, and so wide that it must have been made by driving wagons down both sides of the pile to stack them."[9] By the spring of 1878, the buffalo were gone from Texas. It had taken less than two years to kill millions of animals.

That fall, Quanah and other chiefs won permission for a hunt. They had no idea of the tragedy, nor, it seems, did the officers at Fort Sill. People were overjoyed when the camp criers brought the news that they could go hunting. In the days that followed, they made strong buffalo medicine and danced the ancient buffalo dances. When the great day came, the reservation emptied. Any Comanche or Kiowa who could travel left for the hunt. To make sure there would be no slipups, they had a small cavalry escort.

Moving westward, they watched the sky for buffalo signs. No ravens were to be seen. Nor did they hear the distant rumble of buffaloes on the move. All they found was a vast open-air graveyard. Buffalo bones and buffalo skulls were everywhere. Medicine men prayed, but to no effect. Scouts searched every canyon, visited every stream and water hole, but found only skeletons.

Quanah led the Quahadi back to Palo Duro Canyon, where he found herds of cattle grazing on the lush grass. Charles Goodnight, a former Texas Ranger who had seen Cynthia Ann captured eighteen years earlier, had started the JA Ranch in the canyon; in time, he would run a hundred thousand cattle on a million acres of land. Goodnight gave the hungry band some cattle, and the two men became friends. But no amount of goodwill could bring back the buffalo.

By Christmas, northers were piling the snows deep. The Indians could stay out no longer. Dazed and heartbroken, they returned to the reservation. Even the soldiers pitied them.

✕　✕　✕

The Comanche became prisoners on their reservation. Unable to hunt, their only food came from the government, and it could be collected only at the reservation headquarters. Issue day came once every two weeks. Dressed in their finest clothes,

Charles Goodnight was a pioneer cattleman who set up a ranch in the Palo Duro Canyon after the defeat of the Comanches.

each holding her family's ration ticket, squaws filed past clerks in a warehouse with long counters, like a cafeteria. As each passed, a different clerk gave her sugar, coffee, flour, rice, and salt. Beef was issued once a month, on the hoof, for the braves to kill. *Wohaw* was their word for cattle—from hearing wagon drivers call "whoa-haw" to their oxen.

Wohaw were penned in a corral and released one at a time. As they came out, the braves staged a mock buffalo hunt. Galloping after the terrified animals, they shot them with pistols. Squaws ran to skin and cut them up the moment they fell. These *wohaw*, however, were scrawny creatures, the lowest quality money could buy, and the Comanche went hungry most of the time. Few tried farming, because that was seen as women's work, beneath the dignity of a warrior.

Colonel Mackenzie protested. How, he asked his superiors, could proud men be expected to sit still while their families starved? When his protests were ignored, he sent a stinging telegram to army headquarters: "It is unpleasant to be expected to make Indians behave themselves, who are unjustly dealt with."[10] That brought some improvement. During serious shortages, the Fort Sill commander was allowed to give out army

Issue day on the reservation. Officers' wives watch as Indians line up to get their monthly ration of meat and other necessities.

rations. The official ration was also increased, but did little good. The government's Indian agents were notoriously corrupt, and money often wound up in their pockets.

The People grew fewer each year. A count taken in 1875 showed 1,597 Comanches enrolled on the reservation; that is, only 1 in 12 had survived since 1850. There were 1,382 Comanches in 1884, and 1,171 in 1910.[11] No one, probably, starved to death. But hunger weakened resistance to disease, and there was only one doctor to serve the entire reservation. Measles, smallpox, pneumonia, and tuberculosis took a steady toll of lives. Things were just as bad for the Kiowa and the Kiowa-Apache.

Help came from an unexpected source. In the 1870s, herds of cattle were being driven from Texas to railroad depots at Dodge City and Abilene, Kansas, for shipment to cities in the East. One trail skirted the reservation's eastern edge, another ran along its western border. To ranchers, grass is gold. Cattle driven for hundreds of miles lose weight, and thus value, unless there is good grass along the way. Ranchers found plenty of green gold on the Fort Sill reservation. Each year, they drove their herds along its borders, allowing them to "stray" across. Some even pastured them on Comanche lands, a violation of the Treaty of Medicine Lodge. The army tried to keep them off, but there were not enough soldiers to patrol such a large area.

Quanah's people found a better way. At first, painted warriors would ask cowboys for a few *wohaw* to feed their families. If the answer was no, the herd might stampede in the night or the prairie catch fire. To prevent further "mishaps," trail bosses began to pay for grass. By 1881, they were leasing thousands of acres of pastureland the year round. "Grass money" helped buy additional food and other necessities. In 1885, the Comanche, Kiowa, and Kiowa-Apache were earning $55,000 per year, rising to $232,000 by 1900.

The Texans were generous to chiefs who helped them. And Quanah Parker was *most* helpful. Whenever possible, he used his

Right: Quanah Parker and his wives To-nar-cey and To-pay. As with other Plains tribes, a Comanche could have as many wives as he could afford.

influence to get them leases on favorable terms. In return, they put him on their payroll for fifty dollars a month, about four times the pay of an army private. They also gave him cattle to start a herd of his own and built him a two-story, ten-room house. Known as the "Star House," it was painted white and had four red stars painted on the roof. Other chiefs received houses, too, though not as grand as Quanah's. Living in a house took a lot of getting used to, if one had been raised in a tipi. A house was roomier, of course, but the solid walls would obliterate the familiar sights and sounds. That was too much for one child; he made his mother put his bed in the fireplace so he could look up the chimney at the sky.[12]

In 1886, the government created a special court to try Indians for offenses committed on the reservation. The Court of Indian Offenses had three judges, one from each of the major tribes, who served for ten dollars a month. As chief of the Comanche, the largest tribe, Quanah became the chief judge. His colleagues were Lone Wolf of the Kiowa and White Man of the Kiowa-Apache. The justice they handed out was based on common sense and Indian tradition, not the white man's law. Unlike American law, which stressed punishing the guilty, Indian judges were more interested in the welfare of the victim. A typical case involved a brave who had mistreated his wife. Instead of arresting him, the judges ordered him to give her ten dollars and a gentle horse. Such decisions were not popular with whites; indeed, they found little to admire in the Indian lifestyle.

There had once been white Indians—adopted captives who came to see themselves as Indians. Now the tables were turned. Indians were prisoners and must obey their masters, who would settle for nothing less than turning them into white people living in Indian bodies. Everything that made an Indian an Indian had to go. Their entire culture—language, religion, and nomadic ways—would be destroyed and replaced with English, Christianity, and the settled life of farmers. It was to be a quiet war, a kindly war, but a war nevertheless.

This was not a war waged by enemies. It showed, instead, the good intentions of well-meaning people. Concerned about the Indians' misery, certain influential whites wanted to make things better. These "friends of the Indian," as they liked to call themselves, believed in the superiority of the white race. History, to them, was the story of man's rise from savagery to civilization. And since Indians were savages, they were destined to go the way of the buffalo. Their only hope lay in becoming civilized; that is, becoming white in mind, heart, and spirit. "The Indian," said Herbert Welsh, an outspoken friend, "must become in all respects like ourselves, or else become extinct under the action of . . . civilization which will not tolerate savage and tribal life."[13] Whites knew best. If the Indian resisted, he would be forced to travel the white man's road for his own good.

The war was waged on all fronts. Government agents forbade the eating of animal blood and intestines, hunters' delicacies, since it "nourished brutal instincts."[14] Christian missionaries built churches and tried to wean Indians away from their religious beliefs. Vision quests and guardian spirits, for example, were condemned as "savage superstitions" and "diabolic communications." Tribal dances were forbidden as "the nursery and citadel of superstitious and vicious elements of Indian life."[15] Polygamy was declared sinful. Traditional dress was discouraged. When their clothes wore out, Indians had no choice but to wear government-issue outfits. Once a year, each man received a shirt, pants, coat, hat, and a pair of socks. The pants were all the same size, made to fit a fellow of two hundred pounds, and the shirts were of red flannel. Women received a woolen skirt, a pair of woolen stockings, and twenty-four yards of cloth. Cloth was also issued for making children's clothes.

Children were a special concern; for if the young forgot their heritage, Indian culture would vanish within a generation. To that end, day schools were set up on the reservations. When parents resisted, officials refused to issue food until they took their children to school. Other youngsters were sent to distant boarding

Boys at the Carlisle Indian School. Youngsters of both sexes were taken from their families and sent to boarding schools to make them forget their heritage and enable them to think and act like white people.

schools, of which the most famous was the Carlisle Indian Industrial School.

Located in a disused army barracks at Carlisle, Pennsylvania, the school had a motto: "Kill the Indian to save the man." The moment students arrived, they were given Christian first names and forbidden to speak their native language; they had to remain silent until they learned English. They were bathed, given woolen uniforms and stiff shoes, and their hair cut short. Haircuts were terrifying, since, to the Indian, hair was an extension of the soul, to be cut only out of respect for the dead. Those who resisted, or who broke the rules in any way, might be beaten and have their heads shaved. Boys who wet their beds had to wear dresses.

The course of study at Carlisle included reading, writing, arithmetic, and practical skills: boys learned farming, carpentry and blacksmithing, girls how to be housewives.

Most importantly, they were taught to despise their heritage. Native American history was said to be valueless, because it dealt with savages, not people who had contributed to human progress. Students were told about the Pilgrims, asked to explain why England wanted to tax the thirteen colonies, and made to learn the details of the Stamp Act. They were not told about the new foods—tomatoes, potatoes, corn—their ancestors gave the world, or asked to explain how the Pueblo peoples grew crops in the desert, or told about the scores of Indian treaties made and broken by the United States government. A test marked "excellent" had these questions and answers:

Question: To what race do we all belong?
Answer: The human race.

Question: How many classes belong to this race?
Answer: There are five large classes belonging to the human race.

Question: Which are the first?
Answer: The white people are the strongest.

Question: Which are the next?
Answer: The Mongolians or yellows.

Question: The next?
Answer: Ethiopians or blacks.

Question: Next?
Answer: The Americans or reds.

Question: Tell me something of the white people.
Answer: The Caucasian is way ahead of all the other races—though more than any other race, he thought that somebody must [have] made the earth, and if the white people did not find that out, nobody would ever know it—it is God who made the world.[16]

A student wrote on another test: "The red people they big savages; they don't know anything."[17]

Chief Quanah was a strong defender of Comanche culture. It was all right, he insisted, to borrow the white man's material things. He sent his children to Carlisle, because education seemed the only way for the Comanche to survive as a people. Indeed, he was proud that they could write on paper, and loved listening to one of his daughters play the piano. Beyond this, however, he clung to the old ways. When officials ordered Comanche men to cut their shoulder-length braids, he re-fused, setting an example for others. But it was a tactful refusal. Instead of giving an outright "no," he asked if whites did not wear their hair as they wished. The official saw the chief's point. He informed his superi-

Two of Quanah Parker's daughters pose for their picture at Fort Sill.

ors that Quanah's braids were "just double the number affected by George Washington."[18]

Quanah helped found a Native American religion. That religion is based on the use of peyote, the dried top, or "button," of a small, spineless cactus that grows in southern Texas and northern Mexico. Peyote is not habit forming and has been used by the Indians of Mexico for thousands of years. Unlike alcohol, which excites anger and violence, peyote is a natural tranquilizer. Eating the buttons produces mild hallucinations, a sense of well-being, and a feeling that life is worthwhile. Users speak of brilliantly colored visions, of hearing the sunrise, and of floating in the air. The Apache had learned about the drug during their raids into Mexico, and the Comanche acquired it from them. During the 1850s, some Comanches ate peyote to aid in vision quests. After moving to the reservation, they began to use it on a large scale. They, in turn, taught other tribes about the drug, and its use spread throughout the Southwest.

Losing the War for the Buffalo ended The People's free life on the Plains. Their medicine had not protected them from the whites, and they felt abandoned by their guardian spirits. Peyote made the reservation more bearable. For a while, at least, they could escape into a better world, a world of happiness such as the one they had lost. Every few weeks, users would file into a tipi,

The earliest known illustration of peyote, from the *Botanical Magazine*, 1847. When eaten, peyote causes visions, which Indians believe give them spiritual insights. The peyote religion still has many followers in the Southwest.

where they met a Road Man, or guide, who led the service. Throughout the night, to the sound of drums and rattles, he fed them the "sacred food," also eating it himself. The buttons tasted bitter, and users often vomited before falling into a trance; vomiting was a sign of purification, of ridding oneself of bad feelings. In the morning, when the effects of the drug had worn off, they ate breakfast together, shared their experiences, and parted until next time.

Though not the first Comanche to use peyote, Quanah did more than anyone else to spread its use. Through contacts in Laredo, Texas, a border town on the Rio Grande, he imported thousands of buttons each year; these were sold at cost, not at a profit. Dressed in buckskins, his long braids rolled in strips of otter skin, he was probably the most famous of all Road Men. The chief defended peyote worship by comparing it to Christianity. "The white man goes into his church and talks *about* Jesus," he said, "but the Indian goes into his tipi and talks *to* Jesus."[19] All religions were basically alike, he insisted, if they taught believers to be kind and peaceful. Sure in his faith, he took a leading role in forming the Native American Church of North America. Today, only members of the church may buy peyote from licensed dealers.

In 1890, the Comanche heard of the Ghost Dance prophet. He was Wovoka, a medicine man of the Paiute tribe from Nevada. Wovoka had come down with a high fever that lasted for several days. While unconscious, Wovoka claimed, he had visited the Great Spirit, who promised that a new world was about to be born. He, the Great Spirit, would visit the earth. He would come from the West, bringing herds of buffalo, deer, and horses to restock the Plains. Ahead of him would roll a wave of fresh earth to cover the spoiled land. The whites would be swept into the sea, never to return. Indians who had died would return to be reunited with their loved ones. But the Indians would have to do their part. They had to dance the Ghost Dance. Joining hands, they had to dance in a wide circle moving to the left for four nights every six weeks. No dancer need fear the whites, for the Great Spirit had taught Wovoka to make bulletproof Ghost Shirts of cloth decorated with medicine signs.

The Ghost Dance spread because it promised a better world for people who had suffered so much for so long. In 1890, it came to the Fort Sill reservation. Comanches gathered once again at Elk Creek. But instead of listening to Esa-tai, they danced and sang a song the Great Spirit had taught Wovoka. It was a sad song, a song of people who "push hard" against misfortune:

In preparation for the Ghost Dance, an Indian with out-stretched arms is about to go into a trance during which he hopes to see the spirits of his dead relatives.

My children, my children!
I take pity on those who have been taught,
I take pity on those who have been taught,
Because they push on hard,
Because they push on hard,
Says our father,
Says our father.[20]

Yet, thanks to Quanah, most Comanches rejected the Ghost Dance. Adobe Walls had shattered his faith in prophets. Wovoka's claims, he insisted, were as empty as those of Esa-tai. Those who followed Wovoka "are crazy" and would bring tragedy to themselves and their people. "We have been accused of most everything imaginable except being fools," he said, "and people who know the Comanches have never credited them with that."[21]

Quanah's warnings avoided the disaster that befell a band of Sioux under Chief Big Foot. As the Ghost Dance spread, whites living near reservations on the northern Plains began to worry. Even though Wovoka told his followers not to fight, whites thought the dances were actually preparations for war. Local army commanders were ordered to stop Ghost Dancing and arrest Sioux leaders until things quieted down.

On December 29, the Seventh Cavalry found Big Foot's band of 340 starving and freezing people at Wounded Knee Creek on the Pine Ridge Reservation in South Dakota. Someone—it is not clear who—fired a shot. The soldiers opened up with rifles and cannons. Within minutes, Big Foot and 145 of his people (including 44 women and 28 children) lay dead and 51 wounded; the army had 25 killed and 39 wounded, mostly by their own bullets and shell fragments. Three days later, a baby girl was found wrapped in a blanket under the snow. She wore a buckskin cap on which an American flag was embroidered. An officer adopted the baby, naming her Marguerite, but the Sioux called her Lost Bird. Whites call this tragedy the Battle of

The body of Big Foot
is frozen solid in the
position in which
he died during the
massacre at
Wounded Knee.

Wounded Knee. Indians know it as the Wounded Knee Massacre. Had it not been for Quanah, there might have been a Fort Sill Massacre as well.

Earlier that year, Quanah caused a stir by defending the Comanche tradition of polygamy. The chief was living with seven wives: Weck-e-ah (Hunting for Something), Chony (Going with the Wind), Ma-cheet-to-wooky (Pushing Ahead), To-nar-cy (Straight), To-pay (Something Fell), Aer-wuth-takum (She Fell with a Wound), and Co-by (Standing with a Head.) Each wife had her own room in the Star House, which was kept in order by a white couple hired by their husband. Quanah's wives gave him twenty-four children, five of whom died in infancy. It was a happy family, and two of its daughters would later marry whites.

The government, however, disapproved of polygamy. One day, an official demanded that Quanah get rid of all but one of his wives. That would be a very civilized thing to do, he said, and the chief's example would encourage others to do the same. Quanah did not refuse, but neither did he agree. He answered like a diplomat. "I love all my wives equally," he said. But how, he

Quanah Parker and
Ton-ar-cy

asked, could he call his wives together and say that the white man wants him to keep the one he loves best and send the others away? "You come to my house," he told the official. "You pick out a wife for me to keep. Then you tell 'em."[22] The official was not brave enough for *that*. Things calmed down until, in 1898, he was dismissed from his judgeship on the Court of Indian Offenses.

Meantime, Quanah and To-nar-cy became celebrities. Of all his wives, only she had no children, which left her free to travel with her husband. Quanah traveled widely on tribal business; he visited Washington, D.C., twenty times, making the long journey on the iron horse.

Newspaper reporters were impressed with the couple, and described them in great detail. To-nar-cy, like all the chief's wives, spoke only Comanche. Quanah had learned English quite well, although he could not read or write. Less heavily built than other Comanches, he stood over six feet tall and looked like a born leader. "He is a fine specimen of physical manhood," a reporter noted, "tall, muscular—as straight as an arrow; gray, look-you-straight-through eyes, very dark skin, perfect teeth, and heavy, raven-black hair . . . he wears in two rolls wrapped around with red cloth . . . signifying: 'If you want fight you can have it.'"[23]

At home, Quanah wore the traditional moccasins, breech-clout, and buckskin shirt. A colorful Mexican blanket was drawn around his body in cool weather, and he had little stuffed birds dangling from his ears. During their travels, however, the couple dressed as whites. The chief looked like a prosperous business-man. "He wears a citizen's suit of black, neatly fitting, regular 'tooth-pick-toe' dude shoes, a watch and gold chain, and a black felt hat. The only peculiar item in his appearance is his long hair, which he wears in two plaits down his back."[24] To-nar-cy wore a stylish dress, lace shawl, and hat. In addition, a San Antonio paper noted, "Mrs. Parker wears high-heeled shoes, has diamonds on her fingers, and carries a gold watch."[25]

× × ×

Quanah was able to protect part of the Comanche heritage while traveling the white man's road. Yet he was powerless to halt the growing threat to their land.

Danger came from two directions at once. First, "friends of the Indian" wanted to bring them into the mainstream of American society, which was impossible while they clung to tribal values. According to Henry L. Dawes, an influential senator from Massachusetts, Indians lacked the basic quality that made whites civilized: greed.[26] Dawes and his associates hoped that, by breaking up reservations and turning Indians into private landowners, they would enter the mainstream of American society. Second, greedy whites insisted that the government had been too generous, giving tribes (particularly the Comanche) more

Quanah Parker in
white man's clothes,
about the year 1900

land than they needed. By not using the land properly, they stood in the way of progress. Settlers called "boomers" demanded that the Indian Territory be opened to whites as quickly as possible. "Sooners" could not wait; they entered the reservation illegally, searching for minerals, even carving out farms on Indian lands. Oklahoma is still known as the "Sooner State."

In 1887 Congress passed the General Allotment Act, or Dawes Act, in honor of its sponsor, Senator Dawes. This law said that Indians were to be treated as individuals rather than as members of tribes, and called for the breakup of the reservations into private holdings. The president was given authority to divide reservation lands and allot (distribute) 160-acre plots to heads of families. If any family head refused to select a plot, government officials would do it for him. The remaining, or "surplus," land would be purchased by the United States and offered for sale to whites. The money would be held in the United States Treasury to be used as the government saw fit for the Indians' benefit. The belief was that, until properly "civilized," Indians could not be trusted with money or to make decisions about their own welfare.

Tribes in the eastern part of the Indian Territory— Chocktaws, Cherokees, Chickasaws—were forced to accept allotment first. On a sunny morning in 1889, one hundred thousand white settlers stormed into the area to stake claims. By evening, 1,920,000 acres of former Indian land had been taken by whites.

The Comanche were deeply offended. The idea of private ownership made no sense to people who had wandered the open Plains for centuries. How, they asked, could a piece of paper give a man exclusive use of a piece of the earth? It was impossible, ridiculous, like owning a piece of the sky, or the stars, or the air. All belonged to the Great Spirit, who allowed his creatures to share in them equally.

The law, for once, appeared to favor the Indians. According to the Treaty of Medicine Lodge, the Fort Sill reservation had been given to tribes and not individuals. Any land agreement required the approval of three-fourths of the men of the three tribes—Comanche, Kiowa, and Kiowa-Apache. And none wanted to sell their land or accept allotment. In this, they were supported by the Texas ranchers, who stood to lose millions of acres of pastureland for their cattle.

In 1892, the government sent the Jerome Commission to change the Indians' minds. Its chairman, David H. Jerome, former governor of Michigan, made all sorts of promises. He also made a threat: if the three tribes did not accept allotment, the president would use the Dawes Act to force it upon them.

Given the way the Indians felt, it would have been difficult, if not impossible, to gain approval for the Jerome Agreement. Quanah, however, supported the government, thereby winning over the majority. He did so, not from a position of strength, but out of a sense of weakness. Experience had taught him that, once the United States government made up its mind, nothing could prevent it from having its way. Allotment was inevitable, he believed, correctly. He decided, therefore, to back approval, then try to get a better deal later.

The Jerome Agreement was signed in October 1892, but Congress did not approve it until June 1900. In August, Quanah visited Washington with a six-man delegation to appeal to President William McKinley in person. Their aim was to delay allotment for five years, time to build up a reserve of grass money, and increase the size of holdings to about three hundred acres.

The president had a busy schedule the day the chiefs called at the White House and agreed to see them only during a formal reception for other guests. As the delegation's leader, Quanah was to speak for the others. Before entering the reception room, officials explained the rules. This was not to be a business meeting, they said, but an opportunity to be honored by meeting the president. Quanah was to say a few polite words, not bring up his main concerns; these had already been decided, the officials warned, and it would be rude to raise them once again.

Quanah had not come so far just for a presidential smile and handshake. He ignored the rules. When he mentioned his mission, President McKinley said it was high time Indians gave up the reservation life. That did it! The chief stepped forward, raised his hand above his head, and cried: "The white man not treat Indians right. Indian want five years. Then take land. Want three hundred acres. Hundred and sixty not enough. White man . . ."[27]

He was not allowed to finish. The president's secretary and an official from the Bureau of Indian Affairs grabbed his arms and hustled him out of the room, followed by the other chiefs. "I warned you that you should not speak of that to the president," said the official. Quanah, his eyes blazing with anger, realized that it was finally over: The People had lost the last remnant of the *Comanchería*. The official looked him straight in the eye. "It has to be, Quanah," he said gently.[28]

Once again, as in the days of Bad Hand Mackenzie, Quanah accepted defeat. Still, he was as famous as ever. That fall, Vice-President Theodore Roosevelt came to Oklahoma City for a reunion of the Rough Riders, the regiment he had led in the Spanish-American War of 1898. "T.R.," as everyone called him, was a national hero, and Quanah was pleased at the invitation to lead a group of braves in the welcoming parade. His young men, who had never ridden the warpath, borrowed their fathers' warbonnets and put on a magnificent show. T.R. was thrilled. When he took the chief's hand, it was not for a polite handshake. His grip was firm and warm, like that of an honest man who had made another friend.

After McKinley's assassination in 1901, Roosevelt moved into the White House. Elected in his own right three years later, he invited several Indian chiefs to the inaugural parade on Pennsylvania Avenue. It was like a convention of famous warriors. Quanah represented the Comanche, dressed in buckskins and a flowing warbonnet. Next to him rode Geronimo of the Apache, American Horse of the Sioux, and Little Plume of the Blackfeet. Enthusiastic crowds cheered and waved to their country's former enemies.

Captain Robert Carter watched from the sidelines. A serious wound had forced him to retire from the army years earlier on a small pension. Seeing Indian chiefs welcomed in the capital of the United States made his blood boil. Most of all, he resented Quanah Parker. There he was, Carter wrote, "in the inaugural column with other 'good Indians,' most of whom had dipped their hands in many a white settler's blood on the once far borderland of the West." What hurt even more was that Americans never gave a thought to the heroes of the Fourth Cavalry, "who risked their lives and sacrificed their health and future happiness here on earth in [fighting] the savage Qua-ha-da Comanche. . . ."[29]

The president disagreed. The Indian wars were over, and there was no point dwelling on the past, which no one could change. In April 1905, he took a brief vacation near Fort Sill. T.R.'s idea of relaxation was a coyote hunt, in which Quanah was invited to participate. After the hunt, a crowd of three thousand came to see him off at the railroad station. "There is my friend, Chief Quanah Parker," T.R. called. "Come up here, Quanah." He came to the platform, and the president put his arm around his shoulder.[30]

Some weeks later, Quanah visited a store with two of his wives and Chee, his youngest son. A tourist group came into the

President Theodore Roosevelt, standing second on the right, during the famous coyote hunt of 1905

store and asked about the famous chief. When the clerk pointed out the Parkers, they stared at them as if they were creatures from another planet. Just then, Chee toddled up to one of the women and held out his arms. "I wouldn't touch that dirty little Indian for anything in the world!" she exclaimed, a look of disgust on her face.

"You need not be afraid he will hurt you," said Quanah as he lifted his son. "President Roosevelt did not feel that way and often held him." Then he reached into his pocket and produced a photograph of T.R. with Chee in his arms. The woman gave a little screech and ran from the store, trailed by her companions.[31]

The year 1907 was one to remember. The main event was the admission of Oklahoma as the nation's forty-sixth state. The word *Oklahoma* is a combination of *olka*, Chocktaw for "people," and *humma*, meaning "red"; thus, it is the red people's state. The buffalo also returned that year. Their return was not due to any medicine man's dream, but to conservationists who had raised a small herd in, of all places, New York City. This event, to the Comanche, was more meaningful than statehood. Families camped out on the Plains west of Fort Sill, waiting for the big day. When it arrived, fifteen buffaloes were released into the Wichita National Forest Preserve. It was a deeply moving experience. Men pointed out the buffaloes to their children and grandchildren, who until then had only heard of the mighty creatures. They had tears in their eyes, remembering long-ago adventures and long-gone friends.

For Quanah, it was also a time for looking back. That spring, some cowboys were taking it easy outside a store in the village of Lubbock, Texas. They were swapping yarns when they heard a series of explosions, like guns going off one after another. "Sounds like Quanah Parker's raid," said an old-timer. "Why," another replied, disagreeing, "Quanah Parker hasn't raided this country since the spring of 1875."[32]

Just outside of town, they saw two automobiles loaded with Indians. Automobiles—"stink wagons" they called them—were

still rare in those parts, and automobiles with Indians were unheard of. A cowboy rode up to the lead vehicle, which had an elderly man with long braids in the backseat.

"What is your name?" he asked.

"I am Quanah Parker, Chief of the Comanches," was the reply.

Asked about his destination, Quanah explained that it was a custom of The People to return to the place of one's birth and sleep there for three nights before their life is over. His birthplace was about fifty miles southwest of Lubbock.[33]

The end was approaching. Quanah sensed it, and wanted to be ready. One thing, however, preyed on his mind. He wanted to see his mother.

He could, said a rancher he met at Fort Worth the following year. The rancher, whose name was not recorded, had heard that Cynthia Ann's picture had been taken in Fort Worth after her capture by Sul Ross. He did not know who had the picture now, but there was a way of finding out. Quanah must advertise in the newspapers.

Sure enough, a package arrived at Star House three weeks later. It was from Sul Ross himself. The former Texas Ranger had seen Quanah's advertisement. Yes, he knew who had the picture. And, yes, he had made a copy of it, which was enclosed.

It was a miracle. There, for the first time in forty-eight years, he saw his mother. She was dressed in the clothes of a white woman, and her hair was cut short as if in mourning. In her arms she held her baby daughter, his sister, Prairie Flower. Quanah had known many whites, good and bad. Now this one, who had torn his family apart, was trying to make amends. He dictated a letter to tell Ross "that my heart is very glad, and that it is good toward him for sending this picture, although it was he who took her away."[34]

Quanah decided to bring his mother's body to Oklahoma. Later that year, he located her grave, along with Prairie Flower's, also by advertising in Texas newspapers. On December 10, 1910,

Three generations of Parkers in a photo taken during the 1930s. Left to right: Mrs. A. C. Birdsong (Quanah's daughter); six-year-old Donna Parker; and her mother, Mrs. Don Wilkinson (Quanah's grand-daughter).

both bodies were reburied near the Star House. "Comanche may die today, tomorrow, ten years," the chief said afterward. "When end comes, then they all be together again. I want to see my mother again then."[35]

Perhaps he did. Within three months, Quanah lay beside his mother and sister. He died of heart failure on February 23, 1911. He died, as he had lived—a Comanche. Moments before the end, a medicine man put an arm around the chief and imitated the call of the eagle, the messenger of the Great Spirit.

Quanah's passing marked the end of an era. When he died, the government decided there would be no more Comanche chiefs. Thus, the son of Cynthia Ann Parker and Peta Nocona was the first, last, and only chief The People ever had.

Prologue

1. Rachel Plummer, *Rachel Plummer's Narrative, or Twenty-two Months Servitude as a Prisoner Among the Comanche Indians*, Austin: Jenkins Publishing Company, 1977, p. 6.

2. Don Russell, "How Many Indians Were Killed? White Man versus Red Man: The Facts and the Legend," *The American West*, July 1973, p. 47.

Chapter I

1. Walter Prescott Webb, *The Great Plains*, Boston: Ginn & Co., 1931, p. 22.

2. A. Grove Day, *Coronado's Quest: The Discovery of the Southwestern States*, Westport, Conn.: Greenwood Press, 1981, p. 228.

3. Herbert Eugene Bolton, ed., *Spanish Exploration in the Southwest, 1542–1706*, New York: Barnes & Noble, 1946, pp. 228–229.

4. Martin S. Garretson, *The American Bison*, New York: New York Zoological Society, 1938, pp. 44–45.

5. W. W. Newcomb, Jr., *The Indians of Texas from Prehistoric to Modern Times*, Austin: University of Texas Press, 1961, p. 100.

6. Ward A. Minge, *Acoma: Pueblo in the Sky*, Albuquerque: University of New Mexico Press, 1976, pp. 13–14.

7. Ernest Wallace and E. Adamson Hoebel, *The Comanches: Lords of the Southern Plains*, Norman: University of Oklahoma Press, 1952, pp. 39–40.

8. *Ibid.*, p. 47.

9. *Ibid.*, pp. 31–32.

10. Wayne Gard, *The Great Buffalo Hunt*, New York: Knopf, 1960, p. 22.

11. George Catlin, *North American Indians*, 2 volumes, New York: Dover, 1973, vol. I, pp. 200–201.

12. Wallace and Hoebel, *The Comanches*, p. 252.

13. T. R. Fehrenbach, *Comanches: The Destruction of a People*, New York: Knopf, 1974, p. 334.

14. Clinton Smith and Jeff D. Smith, *The Boy Captives*, Banders, Tex.: Frontier Times, 1927, pp. 97–98.

15. John Upton Terrill, *Pueblos, Gods and Spaniards*, New York: Dial Press, 1973, p. 249.

16. Richard Irving Dodge, *Our Wild Indians: Thirty-three Years Personal Experience among the Red Men of the Great West*, New York: Archer House, 1959, p. 535.

17. J. Evetts Haley, *Fort Concho and the Texas Frontier*, San Angelo, Tex.: San Angelo Standard Times, 1952, pp. 4–5; J. Evetts Haley, "The Great Comanche War Trail," *Panhandle-Plains Historical Review*, XXIII (1950), p. 14.

18. Carl Coke Rister, *Border Captives: The Traffic in Prisoners by Southern Plains Indians*, 1835–1875, Norman: University of Oklahoma Press, 1940, p. 47.

19. Edward Stiff, *The Texan Emigrant*, Cincinnati: George Conclin, 1840, p. 42.

Chapter II

1. Rachel Plummer, *Rachel Plummer's Narrative, or Twenty-two Months Servitude as a Prisoner Among the Comanche Indians*, Austin: Jenkins Publishing Company, 1977, pp. 7–8.

2. Dodge, *Our Wild Indians*, p. 529.

3. Plummer, *Rachel Plummer's Narrative*, p. 11.

4. James T. DeShields, *Cynthia Ann Parker: The Story of Her Capture*, St. Louis: published by the author, 1886, p. 25.

5. Nelson Lee, *Three Years Among the Comanches*, Norman: University of Oklahoma Press, 1957, p. 118; A. C. Greene, *The Last Captive: The Lives of Herman Lehman, Who Was Taken by the Indians as a Boy from His Texas Home and Adopted by Them*, Austin: The Encino Press, 1972, p. 60.

6. Wallace and Hoebel, *The Comanches*, p. 211.

7. Mary Jourdan Atkinson, *The Indians of Texas*, San Antonio: The Naylor Company, 1935, p. 301.

8. Ole T. Nystel, *Three Months with the Wild Indians*, Dallas: Williams Brothers, 1888, p. 18.

9. William T. Hagan, *United States–Comanche Relations: The Reservation Years*, New Haven: Yale University Press, 1976, p. 15.

10. Rister, *Border Captives*, p. 49.

11. Newcomb, *The Indians of Texas*, p. 165.

12. J. Evetts Haley, *The XIT Ranch of Texas, and the Early Days of the Llano Estacado*, Chicago: The Lakeside Press, 1929, p. 10; Lee, *Three Years Among the Comanches*, p. 124.

13. Wallace and Hoebel, *The Comanches*, p. 135.

14. Atkinson, *The Indians of Texas*, p. 297.

15. Jack C. Ramsay, Jr., *Sunshine on the Prairie: The Story of Cynthia Ann Parker*, Austin: Eakin Press, 1990, p. 143.

16. Newcomb, *The Indians of Texas*, p. 166.

17. DeShields, *Cynthia Ann Parker*, p. 32.

18. Wallace and Hoebel, *The Comanches*, p. 124.

19. *Ibid.*, p. 127.

20. Dodge, *Our Wild Indians*, p. 191.

Chapter III

1. J. Evetts Haley, *Charles Goodnight, Cowman and Plainsman*, Boston: Houghton Mifflin, 1936, p. 187.

2. W. H. Leckie, *The Military Conquest of the Southern Plains*, Norman: University of Oklahoma Press, 1957, p. 13.

3. Rena Maverick Green, ed., *Memoirs of Mary A. Maverick*, San Antonio, Texas: Alamo Printing, 1921, p. 44.

4. Walter Prescott Webb, *The Texas Rangers: A Century of Frontier Defense*, Boston: Houghton Mifflin, 1935, p. 56.

5. John Edward Weems, *Dream of Empire: A Human History of the Republic of Texas, 1836–1846*, New York: Simon & Schuster, 1971, p. 175.

6. *Ibid.*, p. 176.

7. Fehrenbach, *Comanches*, p. 330.

8. Webb, *Texas Rangers*, p. 59.

9. Dodge, *Our Wild Indians*, p. 534.

10. Webb, *Texas Rangers*, p. 30.

11. Bill Neeley, *Quanah Parker and His People*, Slaton, Tex.: Brazos Press, 1986, p. 37. A "roundabout" was a short, tight-fitting coat or jacket.

12. Webb, *Texas Rangers*, p. 64; Norman B. Wiltsey, *Brave Warriors*, Caldwell, Idaho: The Caxton Printers, 1963, p. 240.

13. Webb, *Texas Rangers*, pp. 82–83.

14. James L. Haley, *The Buffalo War: The History of the Red River Indian Uprising of 1874*, Garden City, N.Y.: Doubleday, 1976, p. 208. The black flag refers to the old-time pirate custom of flying the "Jolly Roger," a black skull-and-crossbones flag, to indicate that they would take no prisoners. To "give quarter" is to show mercy to anyone who offered to surrender. Most Plains horses stood between fifty-six and sixty inches. Smaller animals were called ponies.

15. Philip Weeks, *Farewell, My Nation: The American Indian and the United States, 1820–1890*, Arlington Heights, Ill.: Harlan Davidson, 1990, p. 53.

16. *Ibid.*, p. 54.

17. Hagan, *United States–Comanche Relations*, p. 13.

18. Dodge, *Our Wild Indians*, pp. 318–319.

19. Major General John K. Herr and Edward S. Wallace, *The Story of the United States Cavalry, 1775–1942*, Boston: Little, Brown, 1953, p. 68.

20. Margaret S. Hacker, *Cynthia Ann Parker: The Life and the Legend*, El Paso: University of Texas Press, 1990, p. 27.

21. DeShields, *Cynthia Ann Parker*, pp. 64–65. The man killed with buckshot was a Mexican prisoner who had become devoted to the chief's family.

22. Haley, *Goodnight*, p. 59; Hacker, *Cynthia Ann Parker*, p. 28.

23. Neeley, *Quanah Parker*, p. 62.

24. Ramsay, *Sunshine on the Prairie*, p. 91.

25. Fehrenbach, *Comanches*, p. 452.

26. Rister, *Border Captives*, p. 174.

27. *Ibid.*, p. 129.

28. Hagan, *United States–Comanche Relations*, p. 5.

29. The Kiowa-Apache were a small tribe formed by the intermarriage of members of both tribes.

30. Carl Coke Rister, *Border Command: General Phil Sheridan in the West*, Norman: University of Oklahoma Press, 1944, p. 54.

31. Douglas C. Jones, *The Treaty of Medicine Lodge: The Story of the Great Treaty as Told by Eyewitnesses*, Norman: University of Oklahoma Press, 1966, p. 79.

32. Zoe A. Tilghman, *Quanah: Eagle of the Comanches*, Oklahoma City: Harlow Publishing Company, 1938, p. 56.

33. Rupert N. Richardson, *The Comanche Barrier to South Plains Settlement*, Glendale, Calif.: The Arthur H. Clark Co., 1933, p. 303.

34. Tilghman, *Quanah*, p. 57.

35. *Ibid.*, p. 62.

36. *Ibid.*

Chapter IV

1. Tilghman, *Quanah*, pp. 68–69.

2. Ramsay, *Sunshine on the Prairie*, p. 108.

3. Ben Moore, Sr., *Butterfield: 7 Years with the Wild Indians*, O'Donnel, Tex.: Ben Moore, Sr., 1945, pp. 8–10.

4. *Ibid.*

5. Fehrenbach, *Comanches*, p. 484.

6. *Ibid.*, p. 485.

7. *Ibid.*, p. 491.

8. Hagan, *United States–Comanche Relations*, p. 80.

9. Fehrenbach, *Comanches*, pp. 499–500.

10. *Ibid.*, p. 508.

11. Haley, *The Buffalo War*, pp. 11–12.

12. Neil B. Thompson, *Crazy Horse Called Them Walk-a-Heaps: The Story of the Foot Soldiers in the Prairie Indian Wars*, St. Cloud, Minn.: North Star Press, 1979, p. 111.

13. *Ibid.*, p. 113.

14. Greene, *The Last Captive*, p. 83.

15. Thompson, *Crazy Horse Called Them Walk-a-Heaps*, pp. 69–70.

16. *Ibid.*, p. 74.

17. Robert G. Carter, *On the Border with Mackenzie, or the Winning of West Texas from the Comanches*, New York: Antiquarian Press, 1961, pp. 294–295.

18. Don Rickey, Jr., *Forty Miles a Day on Beans and Hay: The Enlisted Soldier Fighting the Indian Wars*, Norman: University of Oklahoma Press, 1989, pp. 143, 165.

19. Fairfax Downey, *Indian-Fighting Army*, New York: Scribners, 1941, p. 100.

20. Haley, *Fort Concho*, p. 179.

21. Carter, *On the Border with Mackenzie*, pp. 166–167.

22. *Ibid.*, p. 170.

23. *Ibid.*, pp. 172–173.

24. *Ibid.*, p. 174.

25. *Ibid.*, p. 175.

26. *Ibid.*, p. 176.

27. *Ibid.*

28. *Ibid.*, p. 177.

29. *Ibid.*, p. 188.

30. *Ibid.*, p. 190.

31. *Ibid.*, pp. 199–200.

32. Haley, *The Buffalo War*, p. 170.

33. Ernest Wallace, *Ranald S. Mackenzie on the Texas Frontier*, Lubbock, Tex.: West Texas Museum Association, 1964, p. 80.

34. Carter, *On the Border with Mackenzie*, p. 423.

Chapter V

1. W. T. Hornaday, "The Extermination of the American Bison," *Annual Report of the Board of Regents of the Smithsonian Institute*, Part II (1887), p. 377.

2. Gard, *The Great Buffalo Hunt*, pp. 62–64; Garretson, *The American Bison*, p. 101.

3. Carl Coke Rister, *The Southwestern Frontier, 1865–1881*, Cleveland: The Arthur H. Clark Company, 1928, p. 225.

4. Marie Sandoz, *The Buffalo Hunters: The Story of the Hide Men*, New York: Hastings House, 1954, p. 39.

5. Gard, *The Great Buffalo Hunt*, p. 121.

6. *Ibid.*, p. 120.

7. *Ibid.*, p. 127; Sandoz, *The Buffalo Hunters*, p. 254; Garretson, *The American Bison*, pp. 114–115.

8. Gard, *The Great Buffalo Hunt*, pp. 223–224; Wiltsey, *Brave Warriors*, p. 262.

9. Rister, *Southwestern Frontier*, p. 228.

10. Fehrenbach, *Comanches*, pp. 522, 524.

11. Gard, *The Great Buffalo Hunt*, p. 208.

12. Weeks, *Farewell, My Nation*, p. 118.

13. John R. Cook, *The Border and the Buffalo*, New York: Citadel Press, 1969, p. 164.

14. Haley, *The Buffalo War*, pp. 26–27.

15. Garretson, *The American Bison*, p. 170.

16. Tilghman, *Quanah*, p. 82.

17. *Ibid.*

18. *Ibid.*, p. 83.

19. *Ibid.*

20. *Ibid.*, p. 84.

21. Ramsay, *Sunshine on the Prairie*, p. 104.

22. Haley, *The Buffalo War*, p. 66.

23. Olive K. Dixon, *Life of "Billy" Dixon: Plainsman, Scout and Pioneer*, Austin, Tex.: State House Press, 1987, pp. 158–159.

24. *Ibid.*, p. 167.

25. *Ibid.*, p. 168.

26. Gard, *The Great Buffalo Hunt*, p. 174.

27. Tilghman, *Quanah*, p. 92.

28. Neeley, *Quanah Parker*, p. 96.

29. Wiltsey, *Brave Warriors*, p. 255.

30. Haley, *Charles Goodnight*, p. 197.

31. Wiltsey, *Brave Warriors*, p. 255.

32. Wallace, *Ranald S. Mackenzie*, p. 140.

33. Carter, *On the Border with Mackenzie*, p. 489.

34. Wallace, *Ranald S. Mackenzie*, p. 146.

Chapter VI

1. Robert H. Lowie, *Indians of the Plains*, New York: McGraw-Hill, 1954, p. 230.

2. Wilbur S. Nye, *Carbine and Lance: The Story of Old Fort Sill*, Norman: University of Oklahoma Press, 1937, p. 295.

3. Tilghman, *Quanah*, p. 100.

4. William T. Hagan, *Quanah Parker, Comanche Chief*, Norman: University of Oklahoma Press, 1993, p. 15.

5. Hagan, *United States–Comanche Relations*, p. 156.

6. Greene, *The Last Captive*, pp. 123–130.

7. Hagan, *Quanah Parker*, p. 87.

8. Hagan, *United States–Comanche Relations*, p. 112.

9. Atkinson, *The Indians of Texas*, p. 331.

10. Hagan, *United States–Comanche Relations*, p. 124. After commanding at Fort Sill, Mackenzie was given other combat missions. Promoted to brigadier general in 1882, poor health forced him to leave the service two years later. He died insane on January 19, 1889, at the age of forty-three.

11. Fehrenbach, *Comanches*, p. 549.

12. Nye, *Carbine and Lance*, p. 10.

13. William T. Hagan, "Reformers' Images of the Native Americans: The Late Nineteenth Century," in Philip Weeks, ed., *The American Indian Experience: A Profile, 1524 to the Present*, Arlington Heights, Ill.: Harlan Davidson, 1990, p. 211.

14. Hagan, *United States–Comanche Relations*, p. 185.

15. Hagan, "Reformers' Images of the Native Americans," p. 210.

16. David Wallace Adams, "From Bullets to Boarding Schools: The Educational Assault on the American Indian Identity," in Weeks, ed., *The American Indian Experience*, p. 227.

17. *Ibid.*, p. 228.

18. William T. Hagan, *Indian Police and Indian Judges*, New Haven: Yale University Press, 1966, p. 133.

19. Hagan, *Quanah Parker*, p. 57.

20. Tilghman, *Quanah*, p. 145.

21. Hagan, *United States–Comanche Relations*, p. 191.

22. Ramsay, *Sunshine on the Prairie*, p. 107.

23. DeShields, *Cynthia Ann Parker*, p. 79.

24. *Ibid.*, p. 75.

25. Tilghman, *Quanah*, p. 165.

26. Hagan, *Quanah Parker*, p. 72.

27. Tilghman, *Quanah*, pp. 168–169.

28. *Ibid.*

29. Carter, *On the Border with Mackenzie*, pp. 214, 216.

30. Tilghman, *Quanah*, p. 179.

31. *Ibid.*, p. 180.

32. Jackson, *Quanah Parker*, pp. 222–223.

33. *Ibid.*

34. Tilghman, *Quanah*, pp. 131–132.

35. Neeley, *Quanah Parker*, p. 173.

There are hundreds of books on the winning of the West. Here are a few of the ones I found most helpful.

Adams, David Wallace. "From Bullets to Boarding Schools: The Educational Assault on the American Indian Identity," in Philip Weeks, ed., *The American Indian Experience*, pp. 218–239.

Atkinson, Mary Jourdan. *The Indians of Texas*. San Antonio: The Naylor Company, 1935.

Axelrod, Alan. *Chronicle of the Indian Wars: From Colonial Times to Wounded Knee*. New York: Prentice Hall, 1993.

Brown, Dee. *Bury My Heart at Wounded Knee: An Indian History of the American West*. New York: Holt, Rinehart, and Winston, 1970.

Carter, Robert G. *On the Border with Mackenzie, or the Winning of West Texas from the Comanches*. New York: Antiquarian Press, 1961. Reprint of a book first published in 1935. This is by far the best eyewitness account we have of the army's campaign against the Texas Indians after the Civil War.

Coffman, Edward M. *The Old Army: A Portrait of the American Army in Peacetime, 1784–1898*. New York: Oxford University Press, 1986.

Cook, John R. *The Border and the Buffalo*. New York: Citadel Press, 1969. First published in 1907.

Corwin, Hugh D. *Comanche and Kiowa Captives in Oklahoma and Texas*. Guthrie, Okla.: Cooperative Publishing Company, 1959.

DeShields, James T. *Cynthia Ann Parker: The Story of Her Capture*. St. Louis: The Author, 1886.

Dixon, Olive K. *Life of "Billy" Dixon: Plainsman, Scout and Pioneer*. Austin: State House Press, 1987.

Dodge, Richard Irving. *Our Wild Indians: Thirty-three Years' Personal Experience among the Red Men of the Great West*. New York: Archer House, 1959. Reprint of a book first published in 1882.

———. *The Plains of the Great West and Their Inhabitants*. New York: Archer House, 1959. Reprint of a classic work that first appeared in 1877.

Downey, Fairfax. *Indian-Fighting Army*. New York: Scribner's, 1941.

Fehrenbach, T. R. *Comanches: The Destruction of a People*. New York: Knopf, 1974.

———. *Lone Star: A History of Texas and the Texans*. New York: Collier Books, 1980.

Gard, Wayne. *The Great Buffalo Hunt*. New York: Knopf, 1960.

Garretson, Martin S. *The American Bison*. New York: New York Zoological Society, 1938.

Gibson, Arrell Morgan. *The American Indian: Prehistory to the Present*. Lexington, Mass.: D. C. Heath, 1980.

Greene, A. C. *The Last Captive: The Lives of Herman Lehman, Who Was Taken by the Indians as a Boy from His Texas Home and Adopted by Them*. Austin, Tex.: The Encino Press, 1972.

Hacker, Margaret S. *Cynthia Ann Parker: The Life and the Legend*. El Paso: University of Texas Press, 1990.

Hagan, William T. *Indian Police and Indian Judges*. New Haven: Yale University Press, 1966.

———. *Quanah Parker, Comanche Chief*. Norman: University of Oklahoma Press, 1993.

———. "Quanah Parker," in R. David Edmonds, ed., *American Indian Leaders: Studies in Diversity*. Lincoln: University of Nebraska Press, 1980.

———. "Quanah Parker, Indian Judge," in K. Ross Toole, ed. *Probing the American West*. Santa Fe: Museum of New Mexico Press, 1962.

———. "Reformers' Images of the Native Americans: The Late Nineteenth Century," in Philip Weeks, ed., *The American Indian Experience*, pp. 207–217.

———. *United States–Comanche Relations: The Reservation Years*. New Haven: Yale University Press, 1976.

Haley, J. Evetts. *Charles Goodnight, Cowman and Plainsman*. Boston: Houghton Mifflin Co., 1936.

———. *Fort Concho and the Texas Frontier*. San Angelo, Tex.: San Angelo Standard Times, 1952.

———. "The Great Comanche War Trail," *Panhandle-Plains Historical Review*, XXIII (1950), pp. 11–21.

———. *The XIT Ranch of Texas, and the Early Days of the Llano Estacado*. Chicago: Lakeside Press, 1929.

Haley, James L. *The Buffalo War: The History of The Red River Indian Uprising of 1874*. Garden City, New York: Doubleday, 1976.

Herr, Major General John K., and Edward S. Wallace. *The Story of the United States Cavalry, 1775–1942*. Boston: Little, Brown & Co., 1953.

Hornaday, William T. "The Extermination of the American Bison," *Annual Report of the United States National Museum* (Smithsonian Institution, 1887), Part II, pp. 367–548, Washington, D.C.: Government Printing Office, 1889.

Hyde, George E. *Indians of the High Plains*. Norman: University of Oklahoma Press, 1959.

Jackson, Clyde L. and Grace Jackson. *Quanah Parker: Last Chief of the Comanches*. New York: Exposition Press, 1963.

Jackson, Grace. *Cynthia Ann Parker*. San Antonio: The Naylor Company, 1959.

Jones, David E. *Sanapia: Comanche Medicine Woman*. New York: Holt, Rinehart & Winston, 1974.

Jones, Douglas C. *The Treaty of Medicine Lodge: The Story of the Great Treaty Council as Told by Eyewitnesses*. Norman: University of Oklahoma Press, 1966.

Leckie, W. H. *The Military Conquest of the Southern Plains*. Norman: University of Oklahoma Press, 1963.

Lee, Nelson. *Three Years Among the Comanches*. Norman: University of Oklahoma Press, 1957. Lee was a Comanche captive from 1855 to 1858.

Longstreet, Stephen. *War Cries on Horseback: The Story of the Indian Wars of the Great Plains*. Garden City, N.Y.: Doubleday, 1970.

Lowie, Robert H. *Indians of the Plains*. New York: McGraw-Hill, 1954.

Mails, Thomas E. *The Mystic Warriors of the Plains*. Garden City, N.Y.: Doubleday, 1972.

Marquis, Thomas B. *Keep the Last Bullet for Yourself*. New York: Two Continents Publishing Corp., 1976.

Mayhall, Mildred P. *Indian Wars of Texas*. Waco, Tex.: Texian Press, 1965.

Neeley, Bill. *Quanah Parker and His People*. Slaton, Tex.: Brazos Press, 1986.

Newcomb, W. W., Jr. *The Indians of Texas from Prehistoric to Modern Times*. Austin: University of Texas Press, 1961.

Nye, Wilbur S. *Carbine and Lance: The Story of Old Fort Sill*. Norman: University of Oklahoma Press, 1937.

Nystel, Ole T. *Three Months with the Wild Indians*. Dallas: Wilmans Brothers, 1888.

Plummer, Rachel. *Rachel Plummer's Narrative, or Twenty-two Months Servitude as a Prisoner Among the Comanche Indians*. Austin, Tex.: Jenkins Publishing Company, 1977. Reprint of a work first published in 1839.

Ramsay, Jack C., Jr. *Sunshine on the Prairie: The Story of Cynthia Ann Parker*. Austin: Eakin Press, 1990.

Richardson, Rupert N. *The Comanche Barrier to South Plains Settlement*. Glendale, Calif.: The Arthur H. Clark Co., 1933.

Rickey, Don, Jr. *Forty Miles a Day on Beans and Hay: The Enlisted Soldier Fighting the Indian Wars.* Norman: University of Oklahoma Press, 1989.

Rister, Carl Coke. *Border Captives: The Traffic in Prisoners by Southern Plains Indians, 1835–1875.* Norman: University of Oklahoma Press, 1940.

———. *Border Command: General Phil Sheridan in the West.* Norman: University of Oklahoma Press, 1944.

———. *Fort Griffin and the Texas Frontier.* Norman: University of Oklahoma Press, 1956.

———. *Robert E. Lee in Texas.* Norman: University of Oklahoma Press, 1946.

———. *The Southwestern Frontier, 1865–1881.* Cleveland: The Arthur H. Clark Company, 1928.

Roe, Frank G. *The Indian and the Horse.* Norman: University of Oklahoma Press, 1951.

Russell, Don. "How Many Indians Were Killed? White Man Versus Red Man: The Facts and the Legend," *The American West,* July 1973, pp. 42–47, 61–63.

Sandoz, Marie. *The Buffalo Hunters: The Story of the Hide Men.* New York: Hastings House, 1954.

Stewart, Omer C. *Peyote Religion: A History.* Norman: University of Oklahoma Press, 1987.

Terrill, John Upton. *Pueblos, Gods and Spaniards.* New York: The Dial Press, 1973.

Thompson, Neil B. *Crazy Horse Called Them Walk-a-Heaps: The Story of the Foot Soldiers in the Prairie Indian Wars.* St. Cloud, Minn.: North Star Press, 1979.

Tilghman, Zoe A. *Quanah: Eagle of the Comanches.* Oklahoma City: Harlow Publishing Company, 1938.

Utley, Robert M. *Frontier Regulars: The United States Army and the Indian, 1866–1891.* New York: Macmillan, 1973.

Wallace, Ernest. *Ranald S. Mackenzie on the Texas Frontier.* Lubbock: West Texas Museum Association, 1964.

Wallace, Ernest, and E. Adamson Hoebel. *The Comanches: Lords of the South Plains.* Norman: University of Oklahoma Press, 1952.

Webb, Walter Prescott. *The Great Plains.* Boston: Ginn & Co., 1931. This book is a not-to-be-missed classic.

———. *The Texas Rangers: A Century of Frontier Defense.* Boston: Houghton Mifflin, 1935.

Weeks, Philip, ed. *The American Indian Experience: A Profile, 1524 to the Present.* Arlington Heights, Ill.: Forum Press, 1975.

————. *Farewell, My Nation: The American Indian and the United States, 1820–1890.* Arlington Heights, Ill.: Harlan Davidson, 1990.

Weems, John Edward. *Dream of Empire: A Human History of the Republic of Texas, 1836–1846.* New York: Simon and Schuster, 1971.

Whitman, S. E. *The Troopers: An Informal History of the Plains Cavalry, 1865–1890.* New York: Hastings House, 1962.

Wiltsey, Norman B. *Brave Warriors.* Caldwell, Idaho: The Caxton Printers, 1963.

Note: Page numbers in italic refer to illustrations and captions.

Photo credits for *Plains Warrior*